Fall of Time

Fall of Time

S. D. UNWIN

Copyright © 2022 by S. D. Unwin

All rights reserved.

ISBN-13: 979-8819536070

For Heather, Julia, June, Ethel, and Esther

ONE

First Stop: Bar Avalon, Midtown Manhattan. June 1, 1978 CE

Athos looks at D'Artagnan and taps a watch that isn't there. "We don't have all the time in the world." The others laugh even though Athos makes the joke daily. Athos must have begun his celebration earlier than the rest of them. On the tray of drinks Dart carries to the table is one that's fluorescent green. It's for Athos. They'd picked 1978 because the Green Demon was never the same after Ralph the bartender retired. There's a yellow one for Aramis because she'd liked the look of it on the shelf, straight-up Scotch for Porthos, and a beer for Dart.

Athos raises his glass. "Another total gem. And look—once again we survive to party. All for one ..." They clink glasses and the spillage is a rainbow of booze.

"Yeah, whatever," the others respond.

The place is hopping. Behind the bar Ralph is juggling drinks and cocktail shakers while barking orders at his apprentices. There are knots of men and women around the bar and raucous after-work office parties at the tables, none of them ready to let go of the brief interlude between a crushing workday and a train to the suburbs. At this time of evening in Bar Avalon, the Musketeers could be announcing murder plots through the PA system and no one would notice or care.

"So. Consequences?" Dart asks. It's a piece of business that has to get done.

"Nothing I've noticed," Aramis says, grimacing at the taste of the yellow fluid.

Dart shakes his head. "Wow. I was sure this one would get us."

Athos is grinning. "You're always sure this one'll get us."

"Athos is right," Aramis says. "You're such a worrywart, Darty." She pauses for a second swig.

"But this one was pretty damn good, wasn't it?" Athos says. "*We're* pretty damn good."

Second Stop: Heracles' Taverna, Athens. Third day of Anthesterion, 460 BCE

The wine is pleasantly chilled, fresh from the snow pit. The Musketeers each raise their kylix and take a deep draft, spilling most of it over themselves.

"Look at these miserable shits," Athos says. "They're thinking *Is this why we civilized the world?* Sad old bastards."

Was the taverna a bad choice after Avalon's? Such an energy drop.

"I don't think that's what they're thinking," Dart says.

"And this is like drinking cough syrup. Who picked this place?"

"Stop whining, Athos," Aramis says. "We're celebrating."

Porthos is staring down a patron who looks like they might have invented philosophy. The old man is clearly not enjoying the company of the barbarians.

"You start a fight and you're on your own, Porthos," Dart warns.

"A fight ... with him?" Porthos sneers.

"Yeah, maybe it'd be in the form of a philosophical debate," Aramis says, laughing. "He could probably kick your ass."

"Go for it, big guy." Athos grins. "You could use Descartes on him. That'd blow his ancient Greek mind."

"Like you guys know shit about Descartes," Aramis says, rolling her eyes.

There's a cool breeze entering through the taverna doorway and Dart is enjoying a calm that Midtown hadn't offered. The last thing he needs is for Porthos to kick off; but luckily, the big guy is ninety-eight percent threat and two percent action. And if this turns out to be the two percent, then Aramis will keep him in check, all five feet of her.

"But this place is dull, isn't it?" Athos says. "Let's take it off the list."

"You do know that the Greeks set the scene for all of Western civilization by just sitting around, chugging this goo and talking bullshit?" Dart says.

"Yeah, no one sober could have come up with that crap," Porthos replies.

"So why have you never come up with profound philosophies when *you're* cooked, Porthos?" Dart asks. "You just become a cantankerous big bastard."

"And what good did it do them? What good did it do anyone? In the end, we all understand fuck all," Porthos growls.

"Hey, lighten up, bro," Athos says. "We're celebrating. Think what we just got away with." Porthos smiles begrudgingly. "Okay, date game."

"No," they groan simultaneously. They'd already had enough to drink.

"Come on. Scared of a challenge? Is it because I'm invincible and you know it?"

"But we never know if you're right," Aramis protests.

"Whaa?" Athos affects indignation. "A Musketeer bullshitting his fellow Musketeers?" They shake their heads. "Come on, any number up to four digits—any random number."

"1485," Aramis says.

"Battle of Bosworth Field," Athos shoots back. "My kingdom for a horse." All but Athos raise their kylix and take a swig.

"1294."

"Death of Kublai Khan," he says without hesitation. Another swig for the losers.

"356."

"BCE—birth of Alexander the Great. CE—Battle of Reims. Two swigs, assholes."

Dart shakes his head in admiration. There's no question that Athos has his history down, and the skill seems sharpened by alcohol. And yet Athos has no qualms about the fact that what they're up to could make all that knowledge wrong in an instant, every piece of the history he knows wiped out in a single edit. In theory.

"1430."

Athos hesitates.

"We have the bastard," Dart says.

Then a grin slowly forms on Athos's face. "The penultimate year in the life of Joan of Arc." The Musketeers burst into laughter.

"Are you serious?"

"That's legit," Athos protests without conviction, but raises his kylix anyway.

Third Stop: The Lamb and Flag Public House, London. April 3, 1799 CE

By this time even Athos is winding down. Through the haze of pipe smoke, Dart guesses the crash is one beaker of flip away. Next to him Aramis surveys the room to see who's looking at her. After all this is not the place for a respectable eighteenth-century lady. It's not that she cares, but she enjoys staring right back. This pub was Porthos's choice.

What he likes so much about this era and place, Dart doesn't know, but he always seems at home here, even though he's very far from it.

"We did it. We survived it again," Athos says with a slur.

He's right. And that's the thrill. To still be here. They had pulled off an edit, and they still exist. They will always exist—at least as a practical matter. Because if it ever turned out that they'd de-existed themselves, then they'd never know it. They all lived with that logic: there's only ever cause to celebrate, never to commiserate.

"You know," says Aramis, "I agree with Dart. It's incredible how little effect we have in the long run. Some of those things should have been momentous, right? Should have changed everything, yet ..."

"There is for sure a weird elasticity in the universe," Dart says.

"Yeah," Athos slurs. "Remember when someone edited out Isaac Newton? We thought that'd be big. Huge! But then another guy with even bigger hair comes along and fills the gap."

"It took two guys with big hair to do that," Dart notes.

"Okay, two guys, but you get my point."

"Remember when we were dumb enough to think we could actually do some good?" Aramis says.

Dart stares into his drink. That trying to do good is off the table is something he'd found hard to get used to.

"We vanish von Hayek from the timeline before he was even born, and what happens?" Aramis says. "Hitler, an even bigger asshole fills the gap. It seems nature abhors an asshole vacuum."

"Kaira's right ..." Athos says. He looks up and all eyes are on him. "Sorry." He doesn't finish his point and takes another swig of flip.

When they'd had enough liquor for one of them to make a slip like that, the party is over. No real names. Ever. That's the rule.

Porthos slaps Athos on the back. "Enough drinks, little

buddy."

"Yeah. I was just going to say there are counterexamples. Think of the great Asmus and his edits. He caused the colonists to win the American Revolutionary War. History didn't snap back from that one."

"That one wasn't so straightforward, Athos. There are opinions on that," Dart says.

"Really? You don't think they're just trying to minimize him?"

Dart shrugs.

Suddenly, new life enters Athos and he sits himself up straight. "One more stop." The others groan. "No, come on. This is a special night. It's too early to end the party. Renaissance Florence is calling. I know a place and I know a comely woman in that place."

TWO

Freya hits *Enter* and leans back in her chair. That's another submission deadline met, one that twelve hours ago had seemed like a fantasy. Why does she have to be this way? She'd been in this postdoc position for nearly two years and had never once missed a journal deadline, yet she always convinces herself that *this* one will be her comeuppance—the one that proves she's out of her depth and can't work under this kind of pressure.

She sips a flat soda from a warm can and pulls a slice of meat from a stale sandwich, lowering it into her open mouth. Damian is sitting in front of the only other illuminated monitor in the darkened university office. "Did it," she calls out to him. The only acknowledgment is a brief suspension of keyboard clacking. She knows that Damian Critchley wouldn't have self-doubt, despite never having delivered on time and the quality of what he does eventually produce being shit. It had always seemed so unfair to Freya that stupidity is the best vaccine for self-doubt.

A fly lands on Freya's sandwich. She studies it. If that fly is still there after she counts to five, then she'll get the job. If not, she's stuck with the back of Damian's head for another year. She reaches three and swipes the fly off the sandwich.

Why does she do this to herself? Like there isn't enough genuine tension in her life without manufacturing it. And is this really the way the universe would reveal her destiny—an indecisive insect on a moldy ham sandwich? If there's a classical myth in which that happens, then she hadn't heard of it. Sometimes she wonders if, in some ludicrous way, she enjoys angst.

And is it such a big deal if she doesn't get the job? Most graduates would give up a frontal lobe to be in the position she has right now. How many of her postgrad friends got funding to do research in fundamental physics? This is the Holy Grail. Sure, it's a low-paid, barely respected academic position, but it's the first rung of a ladder. Her fellow graduates are not even within radio-telescopic sight of a ladder. Her best friend sells shoes.

"What you say?" Damian halts his clacking.

It's not that she even knows what the job is. But after being put through a year of security screening, it has to be something quite interesting, doesn't it? She has no faith in this logic, but just thinking about it is more interesting than the job she's doing now.

"Nothing," Freya says. "I'm going home."

Damian waves without turning.

The campus is deserted but for a smattering of students striding with purpose to get out of the cold. Fall has turned to winter and Freya raises her collar to the chilly breeze.

The cell in her trouser pocket begins to vibrate. She uses her teeth to pull off her glove, and then reorganizes layers of clothing to get at the phone. That area code. This can only be *the* call. She grimaces at a passerby, expecting him to share her anxiety.

"This is Freya Beaufort."

THREE

A lungful of cool outdoor air is exactly what Dart had needed. It raises him above the dark, heavy thoughts of the claustrophobic indoors. The sun isn't out but the day is bright under the white sky of thin cloud cover. He walks from the farmhouse towards the barn as chickens scatter from his path. He sees Penelope and approaches to pat her hide of brown patches on white. She looks forward to this every day, and the truth is, so does he. Aramis is calling after him. "Give me a minute," he calls back.

"You know, I worry about you and Penelope," Aramis says from the barn door.

"Well don't. It's mostly platonic," Dart says. He gives the Guernsey a final stroke before leaving the barn. Across the rolling hills, crisscrossed with ancient stone walls, is the tree line of the Delamere Forest. He loves this time and place: 1964, Cheshire, England. The bucolic beauty and quiet calm are in sharp contrast to the whirlwind of risk and uncertainty that is the rest of his life. He had been the one who picked this site as the Musketeers' home.

"They're set up, Darty. Ready to go?" He nods, takes her hand, and they walk towards the old farmhouse with its thatched roof, leaded windows, and moss-covered walls.

The back door takes them into the kitchen. They pass a big table of white oak, with copper pots and pans hanging overhead next to a cast iron oven. Aramis opens the cellar door and they descend a dozen steps to that place where the rural idyll ends. Dart navigates the haphazard arrangement of monitors, servers, and control panels.

"Sit down, we're ready," Porthos says over his shoulder. Athos is sprawled over a plush nineteenth-century chesterfield he had once purloined.

"You're going to love this one," Athos says. "Came over the tackynet this morning."

On the large wall monitor, a New York City street map is replaced by the silhouette of a head, black on gray.

It's a woman's voice. "Greetings to our fellow Allfours from the Spice Girls." Dart shakes his head. There's an unspoken competition among Allfours to come up with the most whimsical name for themselves, which had always intrigued Dart because humor has never been a noticeable trait in their fellow bands. The Musketeers isn't especially clever, its origin pithier than the name itself. *The dumbass universe*, one of the Allfours' mantras, evoked the work of Alexandre Dumas. It's not the wit of Wilde, but then, it's a joke that can never be shared anyway.

"We thought you'd appreciate this," the voice continues, "and wanted to pass it on."

The silhouette is replaced by a grainy image, likely the lobby of a railway station, along with a caption identifying the temporal location as May 1908. The benches are occupied by men, well turned out in suits and ties, and women in extravagantly large hats, their dresses covering them from neck to ankles. Some are hidden behind newspapers, others are struggling to keep children in check. Two younger men are laughing, and a large, matronly woman is glaring at them in unconcealed contempt. The video has no sound, but it's obvious that it was not made with 1908 technology. These rail travelers have an acceler in their midst. The scene is set for a couple of minutes. Dart has seen these things before. They start out slow to get you acclimatized to the temporal frame, then the thing that's going to happen, happens.

Dart's stomach churns. The thing that happens is seldom pleasant.

"Have you already seen this?" he asks.

"Wait for it," Athos replies, and at that moment, a young woman's head flips violently backwards. The image freezes and a caption appears.

Mabel Thatcher. Two gens down, responsible for a malaria treatment that saves 1.3 million lives. The communication is from the Allfours Analytics Team: the AAT. In the vernacular they invented, it means that this victim's grandson or granddaughter developed a malaria treatment. *Four gens down, responsible for high school shooting. Twenty-five children and four teachers dead.*

The video restarts. There's confusion on people's faces. Then the woman who had been sitting behind the victim jumps to her feet, face splattered with blood, and it's clear she's screaming.

A man drops his umbrella and backs away from something out of shot. He grabs his stomach and falls to his knees. The video freezes and the captions restart.

Roger Hampton. At three gens responsible for a traffic accident that kills a woman who, at one gen, is responsible for establishing a democratic African state that supplants a brutal dictatorship. At five gens, responsible for decelerating advances in quantum computing by ten years through setting science funding policies.

Dart looks back and sees Athos grinning. As always, Porthos is unreadable. Aramis flashes Dart a smile as the video restarts. People are throwing themselves over their children, others are running away from what must be the assailant, although they are out of view. Some are frozen in their seats, crying or seemingly too stricken to make a sound, perhaps in fear of drawing attention. Then an arc of blood springs from the chest of a man who's running, and he falls forward. The video freezes.

Donald Redding. At two gens responsible for marrying a woman who, by an alternative husband, is responsible, at two gens, for starting the Hope Victims' Charity. At six gens, responsible for preventing the Central European Fascist Insurgency. Before the video can restart, Dart jumps to his feet.

"C'mon, Dart, the next one's the best," he hears Athos saying as he slams the door behind him.

FOUR

Half of all Freya knew she had learned in the first twenty-six years of her life. She learned the other half on the first day in her new job.

She had never set foot in the state of Washington before, and it was not what she'd expected. She'd expected rain, coniferous forests, a big city, and snow-capped mountains. What she got was a semi-arid landscape of scorched cheatgrass, a cobalt sky, a big river, and a small city with no downtown called Risley. What she got was eastern Washington state.

The ride from the hotel is longer than she'd expected. Small talk seems alien to her driver, which is something Freya would normally appreciate, but this time a comforting chat might have been welcomed. Does the new mystery job have some rule about small talk, because so far, everything about it had been just that weird. She'd always been led to believe that before you take a job, you should learn something about it, weigh up pros and cons, consider if it takes your career in the right direction, then decide. But not with this job. Instead, she had been assured of two things. First, that that's not how it works with this job. Second, that she will, in fact, want this job because those offering it to her, by now, have a better assessment of her than she does. This had seemed believable given the length of the vetting process, which, she had been told, started long before she'd been approached.

They stop at a guard house where the driver shows his credential. Freya, straining to hear what's being said, can only make out the words *new intake*. She thinks of a replacement feedpipe for a toilet cistern. She must be the new intake. They continue across a barren, treeless landscape and eventually pull into a parking lot, next to which stands a single building. A two-story bunker composed of gray cement blocks, no windows, and a single metal door disproportionately small for the building. She takes in the panorama, dotted with small huts as far as she can see. Next to each hut is what appears to be the head of a ventilation shaft. The huts must contain compressors.

There must be something big down there. Something very big.

The tall, slender woman with cropped blond hair holds out her hand. "I'm Jenn Geller. Welcome." She's maybe in her forties, and Freya places her accent as upper Midwest because it sounds a bit like Damian's. "I know you have a lot of questions but they'll be the wrong ones, so it's fine if you just listen and then ask the right ones later."

Okay. Unusual. Freya is used to an environment in which questions are encouraged, being assured that there are no stupid ones. She's always been comfortable with this lie. "But I'll have a few questions for you as we proceed. Come on, this way." It seems Jenn Geller is the no-nonsense type. Freya can live with that, provided the *bitch* boundary remains uncrossed.

She is taken to stand in front of a large window, behind which there is something resembling a control room. It's dominated by a big screen that covers the far wall. Two parallel rows of consoles arc around the screen, all occupied by people staring into their monitors. There's a single elevated chair behind the banks of consoles, Captain Kirk style, which seems oversized for the small, slight woman it contains. The large screen displays a projection of the globe with a dozen little red lights pinpointing various locations. Below each light is the name of what seems to be a company or a university, its lat/long, and another number. Freya tries to guess what the number represents. They range from five to the low hundreds. It can't be elevation because the University of New Mexico has one of the lowest. Employee or student count in some units? Unlikely, unless Ohio State enrollments have nosedived in favor of the University of Western Luxembourg. Temperature? No, makes no sense. Freya turns to see Jenn watching her.

"So? Figured it out?" Jenn says. "Must be unnerving for someone like you, Dr. Beaufort, to see numbers you can't interpret."

"Insufficient information, I'm afraid. You didn't hire Sherlock Holmes." Freya smiles, hoping to take the edge off a typically Freyan reaction, which she immediately regrets.

Jenn looks at her, giving her adequate time to squirm. "Those numbers are acceleration rates, units of seconds per second," she says. Freya returns her gaze to the large screen. This clue isn't helping. Sure, acceleration is measured by a distance or some other quantity per second per second, but what's accelerating here? She peers over the shoulders of the control room operators to find a hint, but that doesn't work. A man looks back at her, as if sensing her attention, and smiles. He has wavy red hair and forty-eight hours of stubble, and he's wearing a white dress shirt, unlike most of his colleagues who are in T-shirts. He turns back to his monitor. "Those are temporal accelerations, Dr. Beaufort," Jenn says. *Temporal accelerations? What the hell does that mean?* "You're seeing the temporal acceleration rates associated with events across the globe." This is an unnerving feeling for Freya: the feeling of not understanding something that's obviously a statement of physics. That has not happened to her in a long time.

"I'm sorry, I'm—"

"Don't be sorry. I'd be shocked if you understood anything so far. Those are temporal accelerations measured in seconds per second. At each of those locations, an object, or objects, are being accelerated at those rates because they've been entrained in a tachyon blast wave. The lights are red because we've been able to arrest the acceleration. That light over Geneva was green a few minutes ago—the acceleration was uncontained. But now it's been neutralized." It seems that this woman Jenn likes to rip off the band-aid quickly. Freya generally appreciates that approach, but this time, it may not have worked. She grasps onto a single word she had recognized.

"Tachyons are just mathematical anomalies, unphysical solutions to equations. There are no such particles."

"Really?" The woman is amused. "Perhaps you're in for a shock."

"Faster-than-light particles?"

"Right—"

"That sweep up objects into temporal accelerations?"

Jenn nods. Freya hesitates before daring to ask the question that now must be asked. Jenn raises her eyebrows, impatient for it.

"Time travel?" Freya murmurs, softly enough that Jenn could think she's misheard.

"Time travel," Jenn says. "Welcome to the Time Management Agency."

FIVE

There's a cold wind on Dart's back as he peers down 72nd Street. The rustling of trees in Central Park is white noise, and above it he hears someone hailing a cab. He's in the shadows outside the reach of the streetlamps, and he begins to shiver. The wait shouldn't be too long because they'd timed it that way. A heavily wrapped passerby surveys him suspiciously. Dart thrusts his hand deep into his pocket, making sure it's still there. Where else would it be? It's always where it should be, but that never stops him from checking, often twice, sometimes more.

That's it. The limo passes him and turns up 72nd Street. It's too dark to see anyone inside, but it's his cue to turn the corner and walk towards the entrance archway. The limo stops. Dart keeps walking, but he needs to slow down because no one is getting out. He hadn't remembered there being a delay, but playing it by ear is what he does. He sees Athos standing under a streetlamp on the far side of the limo, lighting a cigarette. *That guy just doesn't have it in him to be discreet.*

The limo door opens and the woman gets out. She says something back into the open door, then walks through the archway. Dart picks up the pace. On cue, the man exits the limo. He's wearing a black leather jacket over a sweater, so that checks a box. Dart and Athos are each about ten yards from the archway and they're closing in from either side.

Where is he? He should be here by now. Come on.

The figure emerges from the shadows. Lennon looks at him. The assassin assumes the posture of an experienced gunman, holding his weapon in two hands, knees bent. There's gunfire, too rapid to count rounds, and the gunman is thrown against the building wall. Lennon takes a step backwards and stares directly at Dart. He and Athos pocket their weapons and walk away briskly in opposite directions.

Dart looks back before turning onto Central Park West. Lennon is kneeling, the limo driver standing over him. The woman has not reemerged from the building.

Porthos grimaces as the coffee goes down. "That is shit," he says to the server wearing a brown-stained apron, who looks back blankly as if Porthos's words have no meaning. Aramis is in a booth, straw in mouth, smiling back at him. She nods towards the diner door and Porthos nods back. The man who had just entered sits at the bar and Porthos moves over a seat to be next to him. The man doesn't seem to notice. Porthos surveys him with no attempt at discretion, and the man looks back at him until the server asks for his order. He's short, skinny, unshaven, and wearing a sweat-soaked T-shirt.

"Are you Oswald? Lee Harvey Oswald?" Porthos asks.

The man begins to nod before he catches himself. "Who are you?"

Porthos looks back at Aramis with a confirmatory smile. In a flash, he slams the man's head into the bar top who then crumples to the floor. Porthos picks him up by the arm and props him up against the bar. The feckless server has produced a shotgun and is pointing it in Porthos's face. Grabbing the barrel, Porthos pivots it upward and thrusts the butt into the server's nose, who takes a shelf-full of glasses down with him. As Aramis holds open the door for the panicked stampede of patrons, Porthos grabs Oswald's hand and thrusts back his fingers until he hears a volley of cracks, followed by a scream. Oswald collapses to the ground again and Porthos walks away, hesitating when he reaches the door. He has the expression Aramis recognizes as Porthos thinking.

"Was he right-handed?" Porthos asks.

Aramis shrugs.

"Wait a minute." He returns to the bar and picks up an incoherent Oswald by the arm. "Nearly done," he says, repeating the process on Oswald's left hand until he hears him scream.

SIX

The door slams open, bouncing off the wall, and Aramis bursts in, followed by Porthos.

"Did it," Aramis announces with a smile wider than her face. "And we exist. We fucking exist."

"Hell, yeah," Athos shouts, raising his beer before taking a swig. Dart smiles and nods. They had survived another caper.

"Not a word from you, Darty," Aramis says. "You're coming with me." She pulls him up from his chair, through the kitchen, and into their bedroom where she pushes Dart onto the bed. "Get ready," she says, pulling down all clothing below her waist with one mighty tug. Dart is only just in time to receive Aramis in an action performed with surgical precision. Panting, her jet-black hair sticking to her cheeks, eyes closed and mouth open, she keeps repeating "we exist" with each thrust of her hips. Dart hears laughter from the kitchen. Ten seconds pass and Aramis collapses beside him. "Didn't you finish?" she asks.

"I was barely there for the start," Dart says, grinning.

"Oh, Darty." Aramis affects a sheepish smile. "You could have thought of Penelope. I'd have been okay with that."

"Didn't occur to me. It all happened too fast."

Aramis had worked up a sweat, although Dart isn't sure whether it was from the Dallas mission or from the past ten seconds. She rests her head on Dart's shoulder and he strokes her hair.

"God, I love this. All of it. We're invulnerable," she says.

Dart smiles. He knows they are far from invulnerable, but he reminds himself of the Allfours mantra—one of many. *You'll never know you're fucked.*

"You pulled off the Lennon thing?"

"Went to plan," Dart replies.

"What's next, you think? We ready for the Big One? Come on, Darty." She tickles him. "We ready for the Big One?" When an Allfour talks of the Big One, for some it's banter and for some it's real. For Aramis, it's real. She's in, one hundred percent.

Aramis pulls herself up and rests her head on her hand. "You okay, Dart? You don't seem excited enough. How can you be low after today?"

"Oh, just been thinking about the video from the Analytics Team. Couldn't help myself." They'd been over this before.

"Yeah, those guys know research. What about it? It's like a hundred others."

"Those children. Everyone. They were terrified." Dart waits for a reaction from Aramis, hoping it won't be her typical stance.

"There are terrified people everywhere," she says, "all the time, throughout time. But the video made its point, right? There's nothing we can do that changes the grand net total of joy or pain. In the long run, everyone is responsible for the same amount of good and bad in the world. The best of intentions or the worst of intentions or no intentions at all. It's the same upshot in the grand scheme. You know all this." She pauses, sighing. "No matter what we get up to, what we do, the effect is ...?"

Like a patient teacher, she raises her eyebrows, waiting

for Dart to finish her sentence.

"Net morally neutral, I know," he says. "I'm as Allfours as you, Aramis."

"Yeah, but every now and then you need a reminder, Darty. You get so morose."

"Okay, then. Go ahead, Professor Allfours."

She delivers her lecture musically, sardonically. "To reject the idea that time hopping can have catastrophic consequences removes the biggest obstacle to the core principle of the Allfours: the equality of dimensions. There should be no less freedom of movement through the fourth dimension than through any other dimension. We *are* the 4th Movement." She smiles, nodding vigorously. "Say it, Darty. Say it out loud."

"We *are* the 4th Movement," he echoes with a smile.

"And now," she says, swinging a leg over him, "I'm going to take another run at this."

SEVEN

Jenn shows Freya to her cubicle and thrusts a flash drive into her hand. "First things first. The theory. And keep an open mind. Very open."

Freya studies the small plastic object in her palm. Unless this woman is crazy—and this place has a lot of the accoutrements of pure crazy—then she's probably right about an open mind. If it contains a theory of time travel, then an open mind is the very least she'll need.

A woman appears next to Jenn. With her bright green dress, rosy cheeks, short black hair, and diminutive stature, she has the look of a supernatural creature of the forest. Jenn says, "This is Sarah Bari. She's going to help get you settled in and answer your questions once you dive into that drive. A year ago, Dr. Bari was where you are now, so she knows what you're feeling."

Everyone here seems to have a smile for her, even from afar. People are chattering over cubicle walls and there are bouts of laughter. Around the periphery of the room there are a series of whiteboards, filled with equations and diagrams. Freya tries to figure out the scribblings. Some are quantum field theory, for sure, and others look like engineering diagrams, but nothing else is obvious. Jenn walks briskly away towards the control room, leaving her with only the smiling Sarah.

"I know you're eager to see what's on there," Sarah says, nodding at the flash drive. "The files are named in reading order. Let's do lunch." Then she's gone, too.

The sun is high in the cloudless, blue sky. Sarah unzips the lunch cooler and puts two sandwiches on the picnic table. They're sitting next to each other facing the Columbia River, and a gaggle of geese waddle down towards the bank.

"Where to begin, right?" Sarah says. There's excitement on her face but Freya is going to play it cool. If all this turns out to be a massive hoax, then having played it cool will leave her some dignity. But why would anyone put this much into a hoax? Maybe they're testing her credulity to see if she's fit for some other job—a real one.

"The time travel events on the big screen—what were they?" Freya asks. This seems like the right place to begin.

"Huh. I was betting you'd start with the theory," Sarah says. Freya smiles. Smiling seems cool and aloof. "Those were temporal accelerations."

"And who's doing that? And why?"

"The ones on the screen are mostly accidents. The detection array below us sees the tachyons emitted by the acceleration event, and then we neutralize that event. So, if all goes to plan and we catch it early, it never gets to be an actual time travel incident."

"You said accidents?"

"Yeah, you didn't get to the file on tachyonic chemistry yet? It's nature screwing with us. There are chemicals that, if brought together in Goldilocks proportions and at just-so rates, produce a tachyon burst that can accelerate matter. Most events are just hapless, random incidents."

"No, that makes no—"

"Yeah, I know. It's wild, and fortunately they're pretty rare chemicals—didn't exist until a few decades ago, and manufactured for completely unrelated purposes, but yes. You're going to become a chemist, Freya. A tackychemist. Unnerving for a physicist, I know." Sarah bites into her sandwich.

Freya looks for any telltale sign of a wind-up, of a joke, but Sarah just continues chewing. "Okay. So these events are accidents? Unintended?"

"Mostly. That's because the intentional ones are usually well-shielded. Tachyon absorbers."

"Why?"

"Because it's illegal. Well, *illegal* is the wrong word. It's not like Congress passed a bill. But everyone who understands the technology, or even knows about it—and there aren't many of us—is either TMA or ex-TMA. And, as you'll have hammered into you, the ultimate decree of TMA is don't do it. Don't accelerate. Never. *Ever*."

"Why?"

"Well, the chaos. Because of the chaos." Sarah looks unnatural when she's not smiling, and it seems that only something very serious would wipe the smile from this dryad's face.

"So can you stop them?"

"Yes. The first mission of TMA is to neutralize the innocent accelerations. The second one is to stop the deliberate ones, or to reverse their consequences."

Freya looks out across the river and takes a bite of her sandwich, watching the geese paddle out of view behind a clump of olive trees. "Reverse their consequences? How? Through ... time travel?" Sarah nods and Freya chokes a little on her sandwich. She coughs hard, about to pose her next question, when Sarah raises a finger. A solitary walker passes by on the riverbank path. He nods a greeting at them and walks on.

"We can be crucified for having a conversation like this outside TMA walls. I'm setting you a bad example. Sorry."

If this is a hoax, it's a fucking elaborate one.

EIGHT

There had been a sharp uptick in tackynet chatter over the past few months. Dart had noticed Allfour bands showing up that he'd never heard of before. This was disconcerting because anonymity and mutual isolation were the cornerstone of the Allfours' success—of their survival. If one band goes down, there had to be no hard links to the others. But that caution now seemed to have been trumped by this growing excitement. Now, the Time Bombs, the TemporMentals, the Crazy Chronos, the Time Flies, and many other bands are throwing caution to the wind, openly communicating with each other and even revealing their membership.

It's only a matter of time before TMA decrypts their tackynet chatter, and when that happens, all bands will be fish in a barrel. But every Allfour seemed to believe that TMA is an organization of morons, and that any of them with a modicum of gray matter had already defected to the Movement. But Dart knows better. Still, he can worry all he wants but there's not a damn thing he can do about it. Brilliance is one thing—something every Allfour probably has in spades—but basic sense is another. That's a rarer gift. It sometimes seems that the Venn circles of brilliance and common sense barely overlap.

It's two AM and Dart's eyes spring open. He stares at the familiar pattern of cracks on the ceiling. This is getting worse. He has never been a sound sleeper, but now it's like clockwork. Eyes open at two, a worry session, and then anger that points in a hundred directions. Then, if he's lucky, a return to slumber by five. If he isn't lucky, he writes off the night and gets up to make coffee.

He feels Aramis's soft breath on his arm. There has never been an iota of doubt in that beautiful head. It's a good way to be, because being right is overrated. He's known many people happy in their certainty, but no one who's happy because they're right. Maybe it's because what someone believes is part of who they are—it's internal and has easy access to emotions—whereas what's true is external; it's out there in the cold, disinterested universe, oblivious to desires and preferences. He takes a few slow, deep breaths because that's supposed to help with sleep. But it never does. The deep breaths only become a rhythm for his dark thoughts.

It's not that he has doubts about the Allfours' principles. They make sense. The fourth dimension has been opened up to them—not by clever human engineering that tricks nature, but by nature itself. The laws of physics have handed the world a gift. They've offered up time as a dimension for travel, like any other dimension. Tyrants throughout history have tried to imprison others—to restrict freedom of movement. But in the long run, they've failed.

He's forgotten about the deep breathing and starts again. Aramis rolls over and begins to snore lightly. A shaft of moonlight streams through the parted curtains, painting a stripe across her shoulder. He kisses it and then sits up. This night is a write-off.

At times, he wonders whether Aramis, Athos, and Porthos really share his reasons for being part of the 4th

Movement. Is it about liberty for them—dimensional equality? Sometimes it doesn't feel that way. There's a hint of the thrill of ... nihilism. Time is a mystery, but this much we know: if you edit events, there's a chance you'll be editing yourself out of the story. It happens all the time, although not to anyone who's left around to tell that story. Is it the thrill of Russian Roulette—a revolver with an infinite number of chambers? An infinite number of them loaded, an infinite number empty? Is it the thrill of pulling the trigger? Dart shivers and closes the bedroom window. He may as well get an early start on today's plans.

NINE

It's day two when she notices him looking at her. It's the guy who works in the control room and had smiled. Would she call him cute? In a feckless Hamptons kind of way, she supposes so.

Sitting in her cubicle, she watches him approach.

"Hi newbie," he says. His teeth are crooked and white, and his smile is wide. She'll give him the benefit of the doubt. It's not only assholes who use the word *newbie*. "I'm Red Bakker. Is any of this what you'd expected?"

Freya smiles and shrugs.

"What *were* you expecting? Just curious. I like to ask people that. A blind date is one thing, but what they did here is invent the blind job."

He's one of those people who looks you in the eye and can maintain it. Freya has never been that way. There's usually too much premature judgment going on to comfortably maintain eye contact. "Yeah, it's unusual. Didn't know what to expect but was promised I wouldn't be disappointed."

He just smiles and stares. She examines her keyboard. She thinks she wants to get rid of him, but she's not absolutely sure.

"Where you from?" he asks.

"MIT."

"No, where are *you* from?"

"Oh, Brooklyn."

"I thought I heard it." The smile is constant. She realizes that the staring and grinning is what he does when he's thinking up his next question. She decides to relieve him of the labor.

"How long have you been with TMA?" she asks.

"Three years." He has no follow-through, and stares at her for her next question. He seems benign enough. Freya would normally guess that a guy like this is not drawn from the top end of the bell curve, but in this place, that couldn't be true. He's just an awkward, friendly guy, and has no designs beyond that. Because if he does, he can forget it.

Through the large plate-glass windows, Freya sees kids taking kayaking lessons on a small inlet from the river. The restaurant is bustling like it may be the only one in town, or at least the only good one. There are people she'd seen at TMA sitting at other tables. The waiter appears and hands them menus.

"You like wine?" Red asks. She nods. "We're famous for our Cabernets here. Shall I pick one?"

"Sure." She had jumped to judgment on this guy much too quickly. Now she sees that he's just shy, and the crazy-big smile has grown on her a little. It's a genuine smile, not the sort of bullshit one that tells you nothing about what's really happening in someone's head. And besides, it's nice to have some company in a strange place. Brooklyn or Cambridge, this is not. Blue sky, red mountains, green vineyards, and a touch of time travel—she could imagine the trifold from the Risley Tourism Board.

"Are you convinced that this isn't all bullshit?"

"Must admit, I had my suspicions. But yes, I'm convinced. No one I know is going to put this much effort into pranking Freya Beaufort." She flips through the menu. "Just trying to drink from the fire hose right now. Being exposed to an entire branch of physics I didn't even know existed is ... is ..." Is she prattling on? Who cares. "You know, I'd thought for a while that fundamental physics has been stuck in the mud, but I guess I'd been looking in all the wrong places."

Red laughs.

"Worst of all is finding out that a lot of the physics I thought I knew is now roadkill. No, actually that's not worst of all. Worse still is hearing myself say all that out loud."

Red chuckles. "So tell me about your family."

That was a brisk shift. Are they at that stage yet? But okay, she'll go with it. "Third generation Brooklyn. Both sets of grandparents came over from Jamaica in the 1960s. My parents run a grocery store. Only child."

"And a genius."

"I was getting to that."

He laughs again. The waiter returns and pours wine for Red to sample. He smells the cork and tells the waiter to pour. This guy knows what he's doing. She'd read somewhere that only amateurs slosh the wine around their mouths like Listerine. The cork tells all.

"What about you?" Freya asks.

"Oh, I'm from a long line of farmers. But we're still on you. So, here's something I ask all newbies. How old when you got your PhD?"

"Twenty."

"Hmm, not bad but no cigar."

"What's the record?"

"Seventeen, I think."

"Well, in my defense, jobs slowed me down. I waited tables before the grants started coming in—usually the late shift, which was mostly kicking the asses of drunk, ornery students. Built a lot of muscle mass."

Red frowns. "Wow. Well, don't feel bad. I was a geriatric twenty-three when I got mine."

While not in the same league as discovering that the physics you'd learned is all wrong, it was a surprise how much she'd enjoyed the evening. It's dark and the kayaking class has disbanded. With a little Cabernet in her, Freya feels like she could live here—like she could do this job. She spins a spoon idly, balancing it between thumb and forefinger.

"That's quite a party trick," he says.

"Is it? Helps me think; with a pencil usually."

"Will you teach me?"

"Maybe."

He gives her his wide, crooked smile. "I have one too ... a party trick."

Freya sits up straight. "Do it."

"Okay. So, you give me a number of one to four digits, and I'll tell you something that happened in that year." He grins.

"Right." She ponders it. "Seventy-nine."

His shoulders slump. "You don't think I can do it, do you? You're giving me an easy one. That's the eruption of Vesuvius. Now give me a proper one."

Freya shrugs. She really was not trying to make it easy. "1930."

He thinks. "Birth of Neil Armstrong." Freya raises her eyebrows. "You can check it later. That's the only problem with my party trick. There's a lag between me doing it and your being amazed."

"Okay, but I've never heard of him."

Red's smile fades. "You've never heard of Neil Armstrong?"

She shrugs. "Sorry."

He takes out his phone and thumbs something into it, then offhandedly says, "And why should you?"

TEN

The galleon had been anchored off the promontory for a couple of days, so reports must have gotten back to the village by now. Dart wonders what their reaction had been. Fear? Awe? Excitement? It had likely been a combination. This was just another small, isolated village that had no clue what was about to happen to them. And because the Spaniards knew this, they could afford to take their sweet time.

The vegetation is dense all the way down to the river, but for a small clearing on the bank. Dart can hear the voices of the villagers on their way down to the clearing where they must expect the landing party to arrive. They're probably bearing gifts and speculating on what these exotic strangers will look and sound like. Maybe they're gods who can summon miracles. After all, no one who shows up in a vessel of that size could be human.

"You okay, Dart?" Aramis asks. "You up to this?"

"Of course he is," Athos says, grinning. "He's a goddamn Musketeer." Aramis ignores him.

They're sitting in the middle of a small clutch of trees, waiting, their equipment laid out in front of them. Dart knows he doesn't look well and that's why Aramis is worried. It has been a year since the Allfours chatter had started to ratchet up—since talk of the Allfour bands coming together had begun, and the edit referred to as the Big One had become the sole topic of conversation. It was a year in which Dart had gotten precious little sleep, and he couldn't remember the last time his stomach had unclenched. Things were getting insane but he'd kept this opinion to himself, mostly. The tackynet had been abuzz with conversations; Allfours bands, which are supposed to be isolated cells, talking to each other as if they were in a bar—a big cross-temporal bar the TMA could barge into at any moment.

Aramis sits next to Dart. "You look like crap, Darty." He knows he'd passed the lean stage months ago and was now downright gaunt. For him, appetite was the first victim of worry. It had always been that way since he was a kid. "I wish I knew what was wrong. Is it something that bad?"

Dart knew better than to answer honestly, even with Aramis. Reasoned concerns shared intimately have a way of becoming public heresy. He'd seen it happen. "No, of course not. Nothing bad. Just not sleeping well."

"You know, as bands go, we do the good stuff." Aramis seems to know what's weighing on him. "Even forgetting the whole net moral neutrality thing, what the Musketeers do is always for the immediate good. Right?"

Dart nods. If he were paranoid, he'd think he was being tested, but he knows Aramis better than that.

Porthos looks over at them. "We good?"

"Of course we're fucking good," Aramis says. "We're better than good. *You* good?"

Porthos nods. Doubt has never crossed that whirring clockwork brain of his. Wound up by the Allfours now it's just ticking along with confidence, clarity, and certainty.

Athos looks back from the vegetation he has parted for a view of the riverbank. "We're on," he says.

They all move forward for a look. There are three rowboats, each containing about a dozen men. They don't seem to be wearing armor, except for the morion helmets, so they can't be expecting much trouble. For them, it's just a nice day's outing for a little rape, pillage, and contagion. Dart remembers why he does what he does.

"You're going to take to this like a duck to water," Athos says, clapping Porthos on the back. They each pick up one of the shoulder-mounted grenade launchers. "You sure neither of you guys wants to do the honors?" Athos asks Dart and Aramis. They both gesture *go for it*.

He feigns reluctant acceptance of his task. "They're just about in range now," he says, "so let's do it. I don't want them so close that I can smell the bastards. Just get them in your sights," he says, signaling Porthos to get ready. "At this range the grenade will need to arc a little, but the sighting system sees to that. Each round has a ten-meter kill radius, so it'll be hard to miss. Just put the full six rounds into them. They'll appreciate our thoroughness."

Porthos grunts amusement and Athos fires first. There isn't the explosion Dart expected—more of a click and a thud. The nearest boat is devoured in orange flames, and after an instant, Dart hears the blast and feels a mild shockwave pass through. The screaming starts and the conquistadors on the two remaining boats look around wildly. They're probably thinking they misestimated the natives, if they're thinking anything at all. Porthos launches a round, which misses both boats and detonates on the river's surface, blasting the occupants of the nearer boat into the drink.

"Go again," Athos says. With his second grenade another boat evaporates, and the men who had been flailing close to it are now floating like dead goldfish. "Go for another. You need the practice." The next grenade hits the hull of the third boat, turning it into a fireball.

There's now silence but for the crackle of flames. Dart sees no sign of movement; only bodies and body parts being taken up in the flow of the river.

"Nice job, Porthos," Athos says. "Now you've got a new

string to your bow."

"Yeah, nice job," Aramis says. "Now, off we fuck."

As they're looking down at their wrist accelerators Dart sees movement in the periphery of his vision. There's a crack and Athos falls to the ground. Behind him, a short, wiry man with a bowl haircut, wearing only a white loincloth, is holding a stone club. Two others appear behind Porthos, both wielding axes of stone and wood. One of them rushes Dart, causing him to topple backwards and strike his head hard on a tree. The attacker jumps on him, straddling his chest, and begins to bring his axe down. Dart grabs the attacker's wrist and pushes hard. *This is a strong little shit.* The axe continues to descend. He hears a gun being racked. Aramis is targeting the native's head.

"No," he shouts. Aramis pauses, then slams the butt of her gun onto the native's skull. Dart sits up, pushing the unconscious man off him. Porthos has made short work of his assailant, who's immobilized beneath a large boot. The third attacker, who had wielded the club, is gone.

Athos touches the back of his skull gingerly. "Kill the little fuckers."

"No, don't," Dart says.

"Why not?" The question is sincere.

"What's the point of saving them from these European assholes if we're just going to shoot them?" This answer doesn't hold water in the universe of Allfours logic because the native population is as net morally neutral as anyone else. But maybe a concussed Athos would go for it.

"We're done here."

ELEVEN

There are no traffic jams in Risley—this is no Seattle. That's what had been promised. So what was this seemingly infinite line of traffic between her and the next set of traffic lights? *And no rain*—that was the other thing they'd promised about this semi-arid world east of the Washington Cascade Mountains. So there had to be some explanation of why her windshield wipers needed to go full tilt for her to see the infinite line of traffic ahead.

But Freya doesn't mind it. Traffic jams are a time for uninterrupted thought. She thinks back on her year at TMA. Her understanding of the world had changed dramatically, and so it'd been impossible for her not to change, too. And it hadn't been merely a change of the intellect, of knowledge and comprehension, but a more profound one. Learning that time itself is not what she had been taught, and that the great man himself, Albert Einstein, had had it so drastically wrong. It's not just the science either. What she'd learned was at odds with her basic intuition about time. It would have been at odds with anyone's basic intuition.

She pulls into the apartment parking lot and turns off the windshield wipers. The rain thuds against the car windows and the gray outside world is quickly obscured by beads of water and condensation. Is the world out there really as strange as she's being told? She's safe inside the car where, for a moment, she can deny this new reality behind the misted windows and make this a secure place where all her previous beliefs held true. In all honesty, her mind is still not entirely wrapped around this new physics. But then, she'd yet to meet a TMAer who claimed to understand it all.

After a minute, she opens the car door, letting in the cold rain and the new reality.

Red said he'd definitely be home by six, so there's a fifty-fifty chance he'll be in there waiting for her. She has her own key and lets herself into his apartment.

"You're dripping on my carpet," he says, looking up from his monitor with a grin. It's a carpet strewn with rolled-up socks, fast food cartons, and soda cans.

"My drips are the only sanitary thing on that carpet," she replies.

He walks over and kisses her. "Hi, Slayer," he says.

She's now used to the direct, unabashed stare, which this time means he's waiting for the *hi* back. "Hi."

It's a pokey little place, with the blinds always drawn to optimize Red's computer viewing. And there's always a smell that Freya has never identified. Once she'd insisted that they spend a Saturday morning deep-cleaning the place, and afterwards, it had smelled just the same.

"Smell good?"

"What is it?

"Pizza. I got your favorite."

"Prosciutto?"

"They were out of your favorite."

Red serves the pizza and pours the wine. How he's able to live in this tiny dump, Freya doesn't understand. It had made her decision easier when Red asked her to move in with him. She had not reciprocated the invitation, but there had seemed to be no awkwardness about it.

"So …" Red says. Freya senses he's about to launch straight into it. The first few times the topic had been raised, it had been eased into gradually, after a glass of wine, or sex, or both. But this time, it seems Red is just going to dive in.

"So," Freya echoes.

"What do you think, Slayer? A year in this place, you gotta have an opinion."

"That year went fast." She kicks away a rolled pair of dirty socks from under the small kitchen table. "The first half of it was just panic—unlearning, terror, denial. Little stuff like that."

"Happened to us all." Red shrugs. "But you know what I'm asking."

"Yes. You're asking me if I think TMA is misguided and pointless." She swirls her wine.

"Sorry. I didn't mean—"

"No. The truth is, it's complicated and I do have my doubts," she says, Red nodding for her to continue. "I see the argument. Something fundamental happened in the eighties and time sort of opened up to us. I see the point, that anyone telling us we can't take advantage of it is a bit authoritarian, a bit Big Brother. I suppose freedom of movement is one measure of liberty."

"It is." Red smiles in approval. "And you can never close Pandora's box. Once we know how, we're going to do it. It's human."

"We?" Freya says with raised eyebrows. That was cruel of her.

"You know what I mean."

"But I also get the other side of the argument."

Red lifts his glass but it doesn't reach his mouth. "Uh-huh." His nonchalance is unconvincing.

"I mean, if there's one thing we now know, it's that time isn't just a fourth dimension. Old Albert got it badly wrong, right? The universe *isn't* just a four-dimensional image—isn't static in that way. You can go back and change something, and the universe snaps to a new timeline—a new history and a new future—a new reality." She shakes her head. "You know, just saying that sort of thing out loud makes me queasy. It'd be okay if I never had to listen to myself saying it."

"You're dead right. Reality is a shit-ton weirder than anyone thought," Red says, "but that's not the point, is it? It's about freedom."

"But the freedom to risk a timeline edit that wipes out an entire civilization before it ever happens? That kind of thing? Is that okay?"

"Or creates others. Say no one had ever set out for the New World. Civilizations and empires would look different today." Freya has heard this one from Red before, and he always has the energy of arguing it for the first time. "Who's to say it'd be better or worse?"

"Is that the same thing?"

"Seems so to me, Slayer."

"But these are actual futures we've seen ..."

"In one timeline, sure." Red sits back in his chair and backs off a bit, sensing that Freya is noticing his zeal. "And it doesn't take time travel to send history spiraling off in new directions. We probably all destroy and create future civilizations with every little thing we do." The argument has always seemed like a stretch to Freya—different somehow, although she couldn't say why.

"And in an inadvertent edit we could easily vanish ourselves," she says. This was the ultimate counterargument as far as she could see: a selfish and pragmatic one.

Red refills their glasses. "And you know, no one notices a timeline snap, no matter how enormous it is."

"No one but the tuskers. Yeah, I know." Freya had become a tusker a few months earlier—those with the right glandular tackychemistry to remember a timeline before the shift, walking around in their own little bubble with old memories intact. Only a tusker—an elephant that never forgets—is aware of a timeline change, at least if they've survived it. She was not a natural tusker, having learned that there are few of them, so she had to become one through a small jab with the right tackychemicals now and then.

Red surfaces from his rapt attention with a smile, as if remembering that he's supposed to be affecting an emotional detachment from the subject.

"You're not an Allfour, are you, Red?" Her smile is as cold as his.

"You don't have to be an Allfour to love freedom, Slayer."

TWELVE

They hit *Activate* on their wrist accelerators, and without ceremony or drama, the quiet of the farmhouse is replaced by the hum and chatter of a crowded room. Light pours in from a row of small, high windows, creating shafts of illuminated dust in the wood-paneled hall. It's 1893. Of that Dart is sure because that's where the carrier wave of tachyons had been programmed to drop them off. He surveys the people packing the hall and can't help wondering how many of them might be TMA. It'd only take one to end a lot of Allfours' careers—perhaps their freedom.

The physical gathering of Allfours is insanity beyond comprehension, but he knew he needed to be there. There had to be at least a single voice of reason, if he dared raise it. The other Musketeers are all grinning stupidly at each other. They don't seem to be on board with the idea that a room full of Allfours is the very antithesis of how the 4th Movement works, or at least, used to work.

"Incredible," Athos says looking around. "An Allfours convention."

"Relax and enjoy," Aramis says. "We're making history, and not in the usual way. Savor it." Dart manages a smile for Aramis. She's either incredibly naive or just doesn't care. Their lives are immersed in risks, and maybe to her this is just another one.

There are maybe seventy or eighty people in the room and they're wearing attire from many eras and places. A young, red-haired woman, wearing a baggy white shirt and trousers, wastes no time in walking up to them. Her clothing is impossible to date. She looks directly at Aramis, ignoring the others. "Well, we're honored. You're Kaira Prasad, aren't you?"

Dart gasps. "What's wrong with you. Use Allfours handles."

"Here? Now?" the woman replies with a smirk. "Not much point. Besides, I'm excited. It's not every day you get to meet the granddaughter of the great man—the one who pretty much invented tackychemistry ... and TMA." This is obviously meant as a gibe. "You don't mind, do you, Kaira?"

"Use Allfours handles," Dart hisses.

At this point a ruddy, cube-headed man with a buzz cut and military demeanor steps forward. He glares at Dart menacingly. "I think you want to be civil, correct?" he says. His stare bores into Dart, the look of someone whose occupation of the moral high ground would justify any action.

Porthos steps forward, towering over the self-styled Galahad. "I think you want to fuck right off, correct?" Porthos says. The man weighs him up and sneers, leading the woman away by the arm.

"Great start," Dart says. "So these are *our* people."

A slow migration begins towards a line of open doors, and the Musketeers fall in.

Dart finds himself at the back of a lecture theater that slopes down sharply to a desk and blackboard. Allfours are filing into rows of long, curving wooden benches, excited with conversation like long-lost friends. The clothing being worn spans more centuries than these people could possibly have originated from. Since there was no TMA in the seventeenth century, Dart assumes that the guy wearing the knee breeches and stockings is from a band that, for some reason, had chosen to make that century its home. Then to wear that outfit to this meeting was just to show what a jaunty prick he is. Another guy in a nineteenth-century velvet smoking jacket and sporting a Darwinesque beard is shuffling along a bench aisle. *This is what I'm part of.*

The windows along one of the walls are the only source of illumination and they cast stripes of light and shadow across the benches and blackboard, lighting up the dense chalk dust hanging in the air. There's no one at the front of the theater. The Allfours Analytics Team—AAT—imbeciles who had called this meeting must want to make a grand entrance.

And why pick this venue? It's probably so the only options are to look admiringly at the AAT or at the back of the other Allfours' heads.

The Musketeers slide into a row and sit down. Athos, barely able to contain his excitement, is already becoming very chatty with the woman behind him, who's in a medieval princess getup. Dart scans the lecture theater, homing in on faces at random. *Is he TMA? Is she?* It just takes one. The chatter is loud and bounces off the walls, immersing Dart in indistinct babble.

A hush descends as a man enters from the front of the theater. He walks to the demonstration bench. He's big and bulky and his head is shaven. An intricate geometric pattern of tattoos emerges from the top of his plain white T-shirt, covering his thick neck to the jawline.

Barry Te Wiata. It's the only person this could be. So he wound up in the Movement? This guy had been part of the inner sanctum of the TMA establishment, and this is where he ends up? The Allfours? By the time he reaches the demonstration bench there's silence except for the echo of his footsteps.

"My name is Posh," he says in a deep, resonant voice.

There's a smattering of giggles from the crowd.

"Tell me that Barry Te Wiata is not one of the Spice Girls band," Aramis whispers to Dart.

"Just a handle, right?" Dart replies. "But it explains why that's been the band putting out all the analytics."

THIRTEEN

Jenn had turned out to be another surprise. Freya discovered that she and Jenn laughed at the same things and for the same reasons. She had always been led to believe that smart people generally have a good sense of humor, but TMA had provided powerful counterevidence to that hypothesis. Yet, notwithstanding first impressions, Jenn had turned out to be funny and, considering her position, quite laid-back. When it was just the two of them together, the boss to subordinate relationship was put on hold. Never at the expense of seriousness, when seriousness was called for, but telling the other to *fuck off* had turned out to be an effective way of avoiding bullshit and getting to a solution faster.

Jenn hands her a bottle of water. A large oval table of shiny oak is the centerpiece of the TMA meeting room. They're seated next to each other at one end of the table, which is surrounded by twenty ergonomic tilt chairs. A sign above the door in glowing red letters reminds them that the conversation currently taking place is *Level A Secret*. They are alone.

"So, how are you liking it?" Jenn asks.

"You ask me that every time," Freya replies in mock

irritation. "I'm liking it. I'm liking TMA and I'm liking Risley."

"And the shock science? Are you coping?"

"Why? What have you heard?" Freya asks and Jenn smiles.

"I've heard you're one of our best recruits in years."

"And what did you say to that?"

"I asked if we were still talking about Freya Beaufort."

Freya raises a middle finger to her boss. "Truth is, there's a lot I'm struggling with. Stuff I still don't get."

"Like ...?"

"The fundamentals, to be honest. I can make the math sing, but really understanding the implications? I don't feel like I get it, viscerally. You know? Shifting timelines, tachyonic horizon theory, causal looping ..."

"Well, you know that no one really *gets* those things, right? We calculate them and we even experience them. But getting them is something else. Even the great man said, 'We're all apes touching the monolith.' He also said, 'Shut up and calculate.'"

"Did Prasad really say any of that?"

"Probably not. Ninety-five percent of quotations attributed to him are things he probably never said."

"And the other five percent?"

"Maybe half of those are true."

"So what's happening with Red?"

Freya fidgets with her water bottle and says nothing.

"Is he still besotted by his Freya the Dragon Slayer?"

Freya smirks. "Interesting guy, for sure. Lives like a pig though."

"Yeah, I'd guess that. I try not to walk by his cubicle." Jenn seems restless and gets up from her chair to sit on the table facing Freya. "Where do things stand?"

Freya nods. "It's happening. He's recruiting me," she says softly.

Jenn smiles and takes a deep breath. "You didn't sign up for this, I know."

"I didn't sign up for anything."

"That's true. But you were never meant to be an operative. That's a different job description altogether."

"Yeah, it would have been more convenient if he'd hit on an operative." They sit quietly for a few moments.

"And you're definitely on board with this?" Jenn asks.

"Again, you keep asking me that. I'm on board. I'm not completely sure I know what it is I'm on board with, but I'm on board."

"You know, we've never been able to put someone on the inside of the Allfours."

"As long as it's not dangerous," Freya says with a sincere expression.

"So what's next?" Jenn asks.

"He's going to take me somewhere. Said I'll be meeting a lot of Allfours bands there."

"A meeting of bands? No, that can't be right." Jenn frowns.

"It's what he said."

"Where?"

"Didn't say. Should I go?"

Jenn pauses, as if calculating a few moves ahead. "I need to consult some folks but yes, you should go. This sounds like an early win."

"So this is it. We're doing it?"

"It sounds important, Freya. Can't imagine what would be big enough that the Allfours would take the risk of assembling. It seems insane, even by their standards."

"Oh, good. Insane."

FOURTEEN

"Now, you might be interested to know that just one hour ago, Lord Kelvin was lecturing in this very room," Te Wiata says with a wide grin. His voice isn't as deep as his huge body portends. "Welcome all to Glasgow and Bonnie Scotland." A hum ripples throughout the theater. Telling a bunch of physicists that Kelvin had just lectured in this room is like telling a musician that Mozart had just played their piano. Everyone looks towards the blackboard but it had been wiped clean. "We are most grateful to the university for allowing us to use their lecture theater for our little fancy-dress event."

Te Wiata slowly pans the room. "Irregular, isn't it—bringing Allfours together?" *Damn right* someone shouts from the back. "Damn right, yes," Te Wiata says. "But our topic is a big one. Our topic *is* the Big One." There's a delayed smattering of applause. "In Analytics, we're in the business of keeping every Allfour informed. And just as importantly, we're in the business of making sure that you're not *mis*informed."

Where is this bullshit coming from? If they're in any business at all, as far as Dart is concerned it's the business of circulating gruesome videos and spreading bullshit theories.

Te Wiata continues, nodding periodically as if agreeing with himself. "Because when we take action, especially a big action, we need to be in one hundred percent alignment. We may seem like a ragtag collection of eccentrics, and that serves us well, right? What we really are, or what we're going to become, is a well-honed, coordinated collection of operatives who get done what needs to get done." Dart's stomach tightens and he squirms in his seat. This may turn out to be as bad as he had feared.

Aramis grabs his hand and squeezes it. "Hear him out, Darty," she whispers.

"What we need to do here is get on the same page," Te Wiata continues. "That's why I've brought us together. That's why it's worth the risk." Dart's knee begins to pump like a piston. "I think if I asked any two of you what the Big One is, you'd give me different answers." He points to a woman in the second row and asks, "So what is it? The Big One?" She gets the full attention of the audience. Dart can only see the back of her head, but even that looks mortified.

"It's ... it's ..." The theater is totally silent, everyone knowing that but for the grace of god, it could have been them. Finally she says, "It's an edit on the grand scale. On the human scale."

"Hmm. And what is it, this edit?"

"Kill off the common ancestor," she says immediately, her confidence now growing. Dart shakes his head.

"Ha. I see. It's okay that that's what you think. There's been a lot of talk along those lines, I know," Te Wiata says patronizingly.

So this is the guy with the authority to tell us what the Big One is? Dart now begins to rock in his seat.

"Let's consider this idea of a common ancestor, because it can mean different things to different people." A hologram appears above the demonstration bench. It looks like a chimpanzee. "Say hello to Lucy. She's an Australopithecine, in her prime about three million years ago. This lady came down from the trees and took the first step away from the apes. Maybe the most consequential stroll of all time."

Chatter erupts in the theater and Te Wiata chortles. "Good luck finding her, though. Nigh on impossible, and don't think we haven't tried. No, don't get too excited about Lucy. No way of pinning her down."

Dart looks at Aramis who seems quite unfazed by all of this. *Why were they looking for her? This is a doomsday cult.*

The hologram is then replaced by one of a scrawny woman wrapped in animal furs, with matted, black hair. "Now meet Mitochondrial Eve. All living humans descended from this individual through their mother's line. She was stepping out and about around two hundred millennia ago." Dart looks around the room; Te Wiata's audience is spellbound. What might be going on in their crazy heads? How does belief in freedom of movement lead to this? Apparently, under serious consideration is the fucking up of the human race.

There was no plan to do it, or even intent, but Dart springs to his feet. "Why would we do this?" he says, just loud enough to be heard. Te Wiata looks nonplussed. There are calls for Dart to shut up and Aramis is trying to pull him back down.

Te Wiata waves the audience to be quiet. "No, no. That's why we're here, friends—to talk about all of this."

Aramis hisses at Dart to sit down.

"When did this become what we're about? Aren't we all in this because we believe in the freedom of movement?"

Te Wiata maintains his smile and nods.

"I mean, unintentional edits are inevitable," Dart continues, "but we decided they're a price worth paying for that freedom. We started with the intentional stuff, and we told ourselves that that was okay because it's all part of the freedom. The natural order allows it." He'd been saying these things to himself for a year, not realizing until now that it had been a rehearsal.

"I agree with everything you're saying so far, young

man," Te Wiata says.

"And I get the net moral neutrality argument, that everyone in the long run causes equal good and evil, so edits are never bad in the big picture." At this point, it occurs to Dart that someone could argue annihilation of the human race must itself be net morally neutral, and there's nothing quite like seeing the flaw in your argument just before you make it. "But the things we do never result in large-scale, enduring changes. Things that cause history to really change direction are ... social dissatisfaction, new technologies that alter the ways people live. Not the little events that Allfours mess with. We edit out people, but we know someone else just steps in to fill the gap. It just happens that way. History is elastic. It snaps back. And that's good. We can be free without ... screwing anything up." A flood of adrenaline courses through him. "That's good," he echoes quietly. There's silence and Dart sits down.

The residue of a smile remains on Te Wiata's face. "That's quite a speech, my friend." The audience who had turned to watch Dart now look back towards Te Wiata. "What's your name?"

"D'Artagnan."

"Ah, you're a Musketeer." Te Wiata grins. "I'm very pleased you're here. The Musketeers are legendary. The caper where you prevented von Hayek's parents from even meeting was ingenious. Shame about Hitler filling the void, but I guess he makes your point." The audience, as if watching the back-and-forth of tennis, turn back to Dart. "It may surprise you to know, Monsieur D'Artagnan, that I mostly agree with you. Timelines do have this remarkable elasticity and eventually get back on track, one way or another. It's a reason we all survive. That elasticity is a strange thing, isn't it? It's as if the universe has a grand plan and it's keen to get back to it. That's a good mystery to solve." Again, Te Wiata nods in agreement with himself. "Anyway, a question for you, my brave Musketeer."

If there's one thing Dart likes even less than wiping out

humanity, it's being patronized. Aramis knows this and squeezes his hand so hard it causes him to wince.

"What makes you think the timeline's elasticity will suddenly abandon us if we go for the Big One?" Te Wiata asks him.

"You mean wipe out the human race and assume things'll eventually get back to business as usual?"

"Wipe out the human race? Is that what we're planning? I thought I'd just explained why that would be a ridiculous objective," Te Wiata says. "Or at least I was about to."

Dart looks at Athos, who's basking in the attention. No attention is bad attention has always been Athos's philosophy.

"Can I proceed, Mr. D'Artagnan? Can I talk more about the Big One?"

There's a silence and Dart realizes that Te Wiata's question had not been rhetorical. He nods, signaling for Te Wiata to continue.

"Thank you," he says, turning to address the assembled Allfours. "As I was saying, it really isn't practical to search for Lucy or for Eve. That's beyond the ingenuity of even the AAT." There's polite laughter from the audience. "But there *is* something far more practical that's worthy of being the Big One."

Dart is drained and shaky when he returns to the foyer, yet he's also buoyant, as if a kilogram of lead has been surgically removed from him. He's standing tall, and even a lungful of dust-laden air feels good.

Aramis, wearing her typical wry smile, joins him. "Nice job, Darty-boy."

"Thank you," he replies despite the obvious sarcasm. "It needed to be said."

"Here? In front of the first ever physical gathering of Allfours?"

"Where should I have said it? In a cupboard at the

bottom of a mineshaft?"

Athos and Porthos join them. "You have gonads like bowling balls, my friend," Athos says. Porthos is just staring at him, in either contempt or admiration, or a bit of both. It isn't only the Musketeers who have an interest in him. But no one approaches, likely in fear of association.

"Were you worried about there being TMAers here and you wanted to look like a good boy in front of them?" This is quite savage for Aramis, and Athos snickers. Dart had underestimated how upset she'd be.

Athos rests a hand on Dart's shoulder. "Well, you've put the Musketeers in the spotlight, at least."

"Not my intention, Athos."

Athos scans the room, then beckons over a tall black woman wearing a T-shirt with an equation written across the front. Tight spiral ringlets of black hair fall from under her beanie cap, and she looks extremely serious.

"Let me introduce you," Athos says as she joins them. "This is Milady de Winter."

Dart begins to smile but then he places the name. *No, not even Athos is that dumb, is he?*

"Meet the newest Musketeer."

FIFTEEN

Freya wonders how a degree in physics, a PhD in theoretical physics, and two international awards for Outstanding Contributions to the Field of Quantum Gravity have led to a career in which she is about to sign up with a group called the Musketeers. She could be convinced, if in the right mood, that all of this is quite amusing. But what's terrifying is that she's about to do her first time acceleration.

Red secures the accelerator to her wrist, which consists of a touch screen with three chemical chambers and a reaction chamber forming an arm bracer. The three tackychemicals, which until now had been the stuff of theory, are suddenly very real and strapped to her. She's trying hard to take all of this in her stride. Once programmed and activated, three chemicals will be injected in proportions and rates fixed by the controller, and they'll produce a blast of tachyons that'll whisk her to another place and time.

She gets her breathing under control. Why should she be apprehensive about the prospect of an intense burst of fundamental particles, traveling faster than the speed of light, that'll rip her every molecule out of their place in the spacetime continuum and dump them elsewhere? How could *that* go wrong?

"Ah, your first time, Slayer. I'm jealous," Red says. She stares at the numbers on the accelerator screen as Red programs it. "Here's how I want to do it, Slayer. You'll land a little way away from the Musketeers. I want to prep our morose yet excitable friend Dart before I wave you over. You'll see me when you land."

"Excitable? Am I worried?"

"Nah. He's very type A, but harmless. You're gonna love them all."

"And this won't hurt?"

"No pain, no pleasure, no nothing. You'll be in one place and then another. Most people find the actual acceleration a bit anticlimactic. Unless you're the one in a million whose body is ripped apart in the accel." Freya's head snaps up. "Joking. Relax."

"Not fucking funny."

Red seems to disagree. "All set my Freya the Dragon Slayer. Hit *Activate* and you're off."

With a rapid, assertive motion, in the spirit of ripping off a band-aid, she jabs the screen.

Red's filthy apartment is instantly replaced by the bustle of a crowded room. There had been no shock to the system—at least no physical shock—and no sense of the unfathomable thing that had just occurred. She had been in twenty-first-century Washington state, and now she's in nineteenth-century Scotland. The smell of damp and of wood has replaced the aroma of week-old food, the ambient light is gray and natural instead of yellow and electrical, and the temperature has dropped fifteen degrees.

Maybe one day this sort of thing will be no biggie to her, but that's not today. *Fuck* is what she's thinking, so she says it. No one seems to have noticed her arrival, or at least no one cares. There are men and women, young and old, in outfits spanning the ages. Will the Musketeers be wearing the big boots, cloaks and all? Is that how it works?

She looks for Red. He'd said she'd see him, but there are too many people circulating up close to get a good view. A slow flow of Allfours begins moving towards a series of doors. As the number of people in the room dwindles, she keeps looking for Red. This is the foyer of a theater, she realizes. Finally, she's alone and there's no Red. If he isn't there, she has no plan. So Freya picks a door and walks through it.

Carried by the flow of prattling Allfours, Freya exits the theater. She feels fortunate that her capacity for shock has been exhausted over the past year. It's what's keeping her together, because what she'd just heard would have been enough to fling her over the edge. *What insanity!* And all this coming not from an ignorant rabble carrying pitchforks and torches, but from a room in which genius was probably the norm. She feels nauseous, although it's partly because she hadn't been able to eat a thing in the past twenty-four hours. One guy had spoken out in there who seemed less insane than the others, but that was only because Freya had been forced to lower the bar.

The foyer is filling up and she looks for Red. She's sure she had seen the back of Red's head a few rows down. Navigating the groups of socializing Allfours, Freya tries to avoid eye contact and being drawn into conversation with these chatty lunatics. She sees the skinny guy who had confronted the speaker and watches him as he crosses the foyer. He has an unusual gait—graceful and fluid, as if gliding from the waist up. Maybe he'd been a dancer. Then he stops, and after a moment, a group assembles around him. One of them is Red.

They're deep in conversation. One is a petite desi woman—maybe Indian or Pakistani—with long, silky hair that falls down her back. The fourth one is a big guy who towers over the rest like a sumo wrestler in daywear.

Together, they look like escapees from the Island of Misfit Toys. Freya circumnavigates the group to get into Red's line of sight. *Athos, Athos, Athos,* she reminds herself. She needs to refer to him as Athos.

Red sees her and his face creases into a wide smile. He beckons her over, takes her arm, and introduces her by her new Musketeer name. The fluid, skinny one has a kind face, and she could tell that he was about to smile, but something changed his mind. Red introduces his Musketeers. The diminutive Indian woman, named Aramis, has delicate features, flawless brown skin, and a smile of even white teeth. To Freya, she looks like a fragile toy doll that's been made too perfect to be a realistic facsimile of a human woman.

"Welcome on board, Winter," Aramis says. The skinny one looks at the woman in surprise.

SIXTEEN

"This is our room," Red says, throwing himself onto the bed. "This okay?"

"Looks comfy," Freya says, walking over to open the flowery curtains. Through the small, leaded window she sees rolling fields crisscrossed by stone walls, and closer by, a few chickens complaining loudly as Aramis herds them towards a barn.

"Are you ready for what's ahead?" Red asks with a grin.

"What *is* ahead?"

"The life of an Allfour, my Slayer. We're going to find you some *real* dragons to slay. You're an Allfour now and you're going to love it," he says. "Milady de Winter and Athos are going to be the power couple of all time. We'll live in infamy."

"Aren't Allfours supposed to avoid visibility?"

"The times they are a changin'," he replies. "And that's literal." He laughs.

Freya joins Red on the bed. "Did your friends know about me? Did they know I was joining up?"

"Of course," Red replies defensively. "Well, most of them. Dart can be a bit emotional, so I'd been postponing—"

"Seems to me you should tell the emotional one first."

"I figured that once he'd met you—"

"Yeah, well now he's met me. Let's see if you figured right."

Red gently turns her head and kisses her. "He'll be fine. I've known Dart for years. He'll be fine."

Freya gets off the bed. She's in no mood for what she suspects Red has in mind. "That guy, Posh. Is he the head of the Allfours?"

"What? No. The Allfours don't have a head. Or anything like a hierarchy, for that matter. No one would stand for it. That's who we are."

"Has anyone told *him* that?"

"He's the head of the Allfours Analytics Team, but that's just one Allfours band."

"So why was he the one standing up front?"

"The AAT's pretty useful. They've got some real chops in tackyanalytics and they're willing to go through the tedious analysis that no one else is. As far as I know, there's just a handful of them, and they've done more to help us understand temporal logic than the TMA ever did." Freya feels herself bristle but forces herself to smile. "They do a lot. They validated the principle of net moral neutrality. They make pretty accurate forecasts of the effects of edits. It was the AAT who figured out independently how to formulate the tusker serum and now every Allfour has access. They don't lead us but they're fucking valuable."

Freya looks through the window again and sees Aramis returning to the farmhouse. She watches until the woman is out of view. "And the Big One? Did they come up with that?"

Red nods. "That, they did."

SEVENTEEN

"Where's your new Musketeer?" Dart asks.

"Oh, I thought I'd spare her this, Dart," Athos says. "I know you have things to say."

"Yeah." Dart steadies his breathing. He needs to be calm. If there's to be a voice of reason, it has to sound reasonable. "Yeah, Athos, I do have things to say. When do you—when do any of us—get to recruit someone into the band without a consensus?"

"Is that a rule?"

"What? You mean a written rule like all the other understandings we have between us?"

"Dart's right," Aramis says. "You could have handled it better."

Dart looks at her. "Handled it better?" The facade of calm is already dissolving. "Do you get what risk he's putting us in? One TMA operative in our midst, or one recruit who happens to change their mind, and we're all done for. That's it. It's over for all of us."

"I didn't just hurtle blindly into this, Dart," Athos says. "I spent a year screening her, making sure—"

"Making sure?" The pitch of Dart's voice rises, despite himself. "Do you really think that you would be able to spot a TMA operative, even after a year of your expert vetting?"

"Take a breath, Dart," Aramis says. "Go ahead and talk to her. See what you think."

"That's not gonna help, Aramis. I'm no more competent to root out a spy than *he* is."

He glances at Porthos. "What do you think? Give me a sanity check here." Porthos looks taken off guard and just stares at Dart.

"Porthos was completely on board," Athos says.

Dart is about to respond, but now he's being shoved in a different direction. "On board? So Porthos knew?" Dart turns to Aramis, who looks down at the coffee table. "Aramis?"

"And Aramis knew," Athos says.

Dart waits for Aramis to look up, but she doesn't. "So why didn't *I* know?" Dart has regained his composure. The other Musketeers exchange glances.

"Because of this," Athos says.

"Because of what? My stark sanity?"

"Because I knew you'd be pissing blood. Because you've not been yourself for a long while, Dart." Dart's anger subsides and something more subdued, less comfortable replaces it. "You say things you'd never have said a year ago. Someone who doesn't know you might think you're no longer a hundred percent on board with what we've always believed. And you know how dangerous that could be. For all of us."

"So now I'm the threat? Not you for deciding to bring a stranger into our midst, but me."

"Yes, you," Athos says defiantly. "And others have noticed, too."

"Others?"

"Yeah."

"I've been the topic of conversation outside the band?"

"C'mon, Dart. It's not like you've been keeping your opinions top secret. You just got up in front of Te Wiata and gave him both barrels." Dart can only stare in silent incredulity.

"We just want the old Dart back," Aramis says softly. "That's all."

EIGHTEEN

Something awakens Dart. Aramis is sitting bolt upright. The lights come on and Dart squints.

"Who the fuck ...?" Aramis says. There are two men, dressed entirely in black, standing at the foot of the bed. They're big with high and tight haircuts.

"Let's all agree to make this go smoothly, my friends," one says in a bass register. The accent may be Australian. Dart is about to answer when Aramis screams. The men exchange a look of surprise before regathering themselves.

"Get out of our house," Aramis shouts. "Right now. Fuck off."

"Okay, we can do it that way, too. Your choice," booms the bass voice.

The door bursts open, bouncing off the wall, and Porthos enters wearing nothing but a sleeping mask pushed up over his fiery eyes. The second man charges the Musketeer, but Porthos's ham fist lands hard on the intruder's face, making the thud of a car hitting a deer. The intruder drops vertically. The other turns towards Porthos. He's reaching for the holstered pistol on his belt. In one fluid movement, Dart grabs the lava lamp from the side table and launches himself from the bed, crashing the lamp into the back of the intruder's head. The man drops to the ground, and Dart is about to finish the job when a third man in black bounds into the room. Noticing Dart's reaction, Porthos turns in time to slam the third intruder into the wall. He shatters a console table into splinters before sliding to the floor, dazed.

"What's happening?" Porthos asks, only now realizing he needs to position a hand for modesty.

"They just appeared. Thought I was fucking dreaming," Aramis says.

The three men are wearing wrist accelerators. The one who took a blow from Porthos is out cold, maybe even dead. As Dart reaches down to take his gun the third intruder lunges at Porthos, managing to deliver an awkward blow to Porthos's chest. The man jumps back and that's when Dart sees a small black disk attached to his naked friend. Porthos's head and limbs fall to the ground, his torso having vanished. Dart gasps and Aramis shouts something incoherent. The limbs and head, as if catching up with events, begin to bleed out onto the floorboards.

There's a gun pointed at Dart's head. He's panting and starts to shake. For an instant, Porthos's eyes are wide open, staring uncomprehendingly up at Dart, his lower lip trying to form words.

A short-charged accelerator. He'd never seen one used before—a chemically undercharged accelerator with its small tachyon blast radius grotesquely designed to exclude part of the body. Next to him Aramis is wide-eyed, hand over mouth, staring at the remains of their friend.

NINETEEN

It's the scream that wakes Freya. "What the hell?"

Athos stirs. "That's not normal," he mumbles.

"It's Aramis," Freya says, turning on the bedside lamp. "I didn't dream that."

"Okay, okay. Let me think," Red says, rubbing his eyes.

"Think?" Freya swings her legs over the side of the bed, but Red grabs her arm to stop her.

There's loud clatter and banging from a nearby room.

"I don't want to put you in danger," Red says.

"Since when? You couldn't have put me in much more danger short of strapping explosives to my ass." Freya shakes off his grip and pads quietly to the bedroom door.

Red follows and pulls her back. "Wait." Pistol in hand, he opens the door gingerly and looks out around the corner into the hallway. Freya slides past him in time to see someone dressed in black entering the next bedroom. Back against the wall, Red begins to tread slowly down the hallway. There's a heavy thud against the other side of the wall that stops Red in his tracks. Freya stares at him. *You just going to hang there, like a painting of an asshole?* She runs past him and looks into the bedroom. A man who's holding a gun to Dart's head flashes a look at her before turning to Aramis.

"Come here," he shouts at her. With hands and feet in frantic motion, Aramis pushes herself up to the top of the bed. "Now!" he yells, banging the barrel of his handgun into Dart's temple.

"You drop the fucking gun right now," Freya hears Red shout from behind her.

The intruder and Dart pop out of existence. Freya looks down to see two more men dressed in black, one hunched over the other, and then they also vanish. Aramis is sitting at the top of the bed, unblinking. Only then does Freya notice the pool of blood, and she steps backward as it spreads to her toes. She sees islands in the lake of red. She stares at them, at first without recognition. Then she cries out as she backs into Red.

TWENTY

Dart squints in the bright sunlight. He's done a thousand accels before and so there's no disorientation, but maybe his abductor is a little shakier. This is Dart's calculation as he reaches for the gun in his face, but the thug pushes him back effortlessly and Dart lands on a bed of rocks that spike his elbows and ass. By the time he sits up, he's alone. A deep wave of nausea forms in his stomach and bubbles up through his esophagus as it occurs to him that his friend's bleeding torso may be close by. He looks around, heart thudding against his ribs. There's no blood, no torso. He's on a craggy beach of large black rocks and gray pebbles underlain by dark wet sand. He's partly blinded by the intense sunlight reflecting off the surface of the water, which could be a lake or a river.

Then, through the haze, he sees it. On the far shore, maybe a mile away, there's what looks like a cityscape. The reflected light makes it difficult to see any detail other than the general shape of the skyline. It isn't a city of skyscrapers, but of smaller buildings, maybe two or three stories—about ten of them along the shore. Beyond the city, rising into low clouds, are hills covered in dense forest.

The first thing is figure out temporal location is what Dart's TMA training had taught him, although he'd never been on board with the idea that the first thing to do was something other than making sure you'll survive the next fifteen seconds. It definitely looks like a city of some sort. It's not a Viking village or a Greek polis or a neolithic settlement, and something about the regularity of the structures and their right-angledness gives it a twentieth-century look, maybe even later. He looks for any clue of architectural detail, but the haze is too thick and the reflected light off the water's surface is blinding.

He spins around, having realized that he'd been completely off his guard. So that was TMA's second rule violated. Behind him is a forested slope rising sharply from the shore. If it contains threats, they're not visible. Other than leaves flittering in the cool breeze, there's no sign of motion.

Dart hears it before he sees it. A motor, amplified by the echoes off the incline behind him. Shielding his eyes, he makes out a vessel approaching across the still, glittering water. Dart crouches, realizing that the sun blinding him will also make him stand out clearly to whoever is approaching. *Threats in a boat. What could they be?* Almost anything. Most threats could fit in a boat. But as it gets closer, he sees that it's a small boat, and in it is someone waving at him.

TWENTY-ONE

They sit in silence, occasionally looking up at each other, waiting for someone to speak.

"Porthos," Red whispers, as if the word escaped from an unshared thought.

Aramis is shivering. "I've never seen a short-charge used before," she says. "It's fucking horrible."

Freya looks back towards the bedroom they had just spent an hour trying to clean. She closes her eyes and sees the dismembered head—its expression of confusion.

"TMA?" Athos says.

"Does TMA behave that way?" Freya asks. She hopes she knows the answer.

"Allfours?" Athos says.

"Who else is there?" says Aramis. "But which Allfours? Any band could have taken it on themselves to deal with Dart."

"You think they're going to kill him?" Athos says, showing more curiosity than concern.

"No," Freya says looking at Aramis. "If they were going to kill him, they would have done it right here. At least one of them had a gun."

Aramis nods. "Where do we even begin?"

"You know," Freya says, "I'm an outsider and maybe see things you don't, but that guy, Posh, looked and talked like he was in charge."

"Barry Te Wiata," Aramis says. "That's his name."

"Right. Screw handles. What's the point anymore?" Red says. "Everything's changing." Aramis nods and extends her hand to Freya.

"Kaira Prasad." It's mid-handshake that Freya catches up with what she had just heard.

"Prasad?"

"My grandfather."

"Shit."

"Yup. Sometimes it can be."

Freya looks at Aramis—at Kaira. She had just spent a year reading papers and reports, precious few of which didn't have 'R. Prasad' as their first citation. This woman is tackyroyalty. And yet here she is, part of an organization bent on overturning all that TMA and its founder had built. Freya realizes that she hasn't let go of her hand and quickly releases her grip.

"You know, Te Wiata was way up in the TMA organization before he got religion," Red says. "I'd like to think Prasad himself would have seen the light, eventually."

"Yeah, right, that would have happened," Kaira says.

"Instead, he leaves TMA to a generation of insects—tiny drones who just do what they're programmed to do without a thought in their little brains about what's right or wrong."

Kaira ignores Red. "How do you think they found us?"

"The AAT has resources," Red says.

"You mean technology or people resources?"

"Technology."

"And you think they'd have some way of pinpointing the very room we're sleeping in with this technology?" Kaira asks.

Red shrugs. "So what did you mean by 'people'? Are you saying one of us—"

"I'm not saying anything. I'm just trying to figure out

how those two bastards appeared at the foot of our bed. That's accuracy in need of an explanation."

Freya nods. "They say anything?"

"Just asshole thug talk. Wait ... Australian. I remember thinking he sounded Australian."

"I could never tell the difference between an Australian and a New Zealand accent," Freya says, "until a Kiwi friend swore at me in both accents for comparison."

Kaira's eyes widen. "Te Wiata?"

"Maybe. Not much to go on, but maybe."

"Wow, listen to Holmes and Watson here," Red says. "Based on thinking you maybe heard an accent in that panicked instant, you arrive at Te Wiata?"

"Fuck you, Athos," Kaira says. "It's something at least."

"I agree with Kaira," Freya says.

"You mean you think that's really something to go on?" he asks.

"No, I mean *fuck you*," Freya replies.

"Athos," Kaira says, "be useful and get Te Wiata on the tackynet. Should be easy. Ask for Posh."

TWENTY-TWO

"You waiting for me to wade over and give you a piggyback?" the woman asks. "C'mon. It'll barely wet your bony knees, Lanky." The woman is leaning on the boat's steering column and directing her wide, white-toothed grin at Dart. With an urgent thought, he looks down and is relieved to find that his sleepwear had included sweat shorts. He has no accelerator, no clue where he is, and most saliently, no better plan, so he wades towards the boat, and the woman holds out her hand to pull him on board. The water is icy-cold and his bare feet are being spiked by rocks, so walking with grace and dignity is out of the question.

The woman has blond hair that rests on her tanned shoulders. She's wearing sunglasses, and her face relaxes to a natural smile. Between her Bermuda shorts and yellow-striped tank top, there's a pistol tucked into her belt. "Oh, that's just in case you misbehave. Like you'd misbehave for me."

Dart sits in the aft seat and the boat turns towards the city on the far shore. "Where are we?" he asks.

"Oh, I'm not programmed to answer questions. I'm just the lowly skipper of a small seafaring vessel," she says over her shoulder.

"Well, at least tell me *when* we are."

"That would be another question, wouldn't it?" She opens the throttle and Dart is thrust back into his seat. "When do you *think* we are?" she shouts over the engine roar.

He looks at the city skyline ahead. "Twentieth? Twenty-first?" he shouts back.

"Based on what?"

"Those buildings."

"Ah, I see. Well, you're on the wrong track there, Lanky. Those buildings are about as anachronistic as you can get."

As they approach the far shore, the structures begin to emerge from the haze. There's a large building in the center, maybe two stories high. There's no clue as to what's inside, but it looks like an office block. Next, he can make out a few smaller structures, about the same height as the central building, but with no windows. They remind him of the TMA bunkers he'd spent too much time in. As they get closer still, the buildings around the periphery of the site look like military barracks—rows of small one-story buildings, all painted dark gray.

In the forecourt of the windowed building is a Doric column with a large red apple sitting on top. This seems like a different variety of strange.

"Why is there an apple in front of that building?" Dart asks. "Can you answer that one?"

"It's a tomato."

"Why is there a tomato in front of that building?"

"You ask intriguing questions, lanky one." Under different circumstances, Dart would have found this woman attractive, even funny, but given the current situation, he does not find her funny. There are people onshore, walking between buildings, sitting on benches, talking in groups, and generally getting on with their lives. Attire looks twentieth and twenty-first century, although Dart has traveled enough to forget which is which. There's a small pier with a man obviously awaiting Dart's arrival. He guesses that the man is well-armed and unlikely to be as flirtatious as this skipper. Within a couple of minutes the boat is guided parallel to the pier with well-practiced ease. The man walks towards them and Dart squints in the sunlight to make out his features.

"Joad," Dart says to his father.

TWENTY-THREE

The screen is blank even though the agreed time for the meeting had passed five minutes ago.

Freya smiles at Kaira. "He's a busy guy, I'm sure. Or just one of those assholes who thinks being late gives him the upper hand."

"Yeah, chill," Red adds.

"Shut up, Red," Kaira says. He doesn't look offended. This must be how Kaira communicates with him, and Freya can sort of understand why. If there's just the right thing to say, Red has always been able to figure out its exact opposite.

"You sure it was—" Kaira begins when the screen fills with color.

"Kaira," says the big, meaty face that has just appeared. "So sorry I'm late."

"Oh, that's fi—"

"Just let me look at you for a minute," he says. He smiles and shakes his head. "You know, I've known you since you were a toddler. Let me take you in." He's wearing a sleeveless T-shirt that displays the intricate web of tattoos covering his arms and neck, and a smile covers his huge face. "Sorry if that's rude."

"No, that's—"

"I used to call you Kia Ora. That was your Kiwi name. Do you remember that?"

"I was little."

"It used to make Ram chuckle," he says and begins to laugh. Freya had never heard anyone refer to Prasad by his first name. It was obviously meant to impress. Te Wiata appears to be sitting in a regular family kitchen overlooking a well-tended garden of exotic, colorful flowers, but it's not possible to tell whether the backdrop is real. "So who do you have with you, Kaira?"

Kaira looks momentarily surprised by the question, as if she had forgotten she's not alone.

"This is Athos and—"

"Kaira, I think the time has passed for handles," Te Wiata says. "Things are changing, don't you think?" Freya remembers that Red had said exactly the same thing.

"Yes, they are," Kaira replies. "This is ..." She looks at Red, her eyes momentarily blank.

"Red," Freya says.

"Yes, Red. And this is Freya, our latest recruit."

Te Wiata studies Freya for a moment. "Good. We need new recruits. Smart ones. Welcome, Freya." This guy is the kind of friendly that can't be real. It's all too big and intense. Or is this the New York flavor of hard-ass cynicism she's been trying to subdue for the past few years? She's read about people who are genuinely friendly, but they generally live in places she has never visited.

"So, Kaira, is there something I can help you with?" His sudden transition to business takes Freya off guard.

"Eh, well, yes," Kaira replies. "I had no way of finding you before, Dr. Te Wiata. Somehow, I didn't connect the dots between you and Posh." Kaira seems to be responding to an unmade point.

This earns Kaira a hearty guffaw. "Barry. I'm Barry to Ram's granddaughter."

Kaira takes a breath. "One of our team has been taken."

"Taken? By who?"

"Don't know. Three thugs acceled into our home and popped him out. But not before they short-charged another Musketeer."

Te Wiata displays shock. "Short-charged? That's appalling."

"Yes."

"And the teammate they acceled?"

"You've actually spoken to him." Te Wiata looks nonplussed. "You remember the Musketeer who stood up in Glasgow and shared a few concerns?"

Te Wiata pauses and pretends to think for a moment. "Ah yes, I do. Him?"

"Yes, him."

"A very thoughtful guy." Te Wiata looks sideways as if his attention has been distracted. He nods to whoever is off-screen and then returns his attention to Kaira. "And you want me to help you locate him?"

"Yes, please," Kaira replies.

Or just hand him back to us, Freya thinks.

Te Wiata smiles warmly. "Of course, Kaira. I'll do everything I can." Kaira flashes a smile on and off at him. "You know, I'm sorry these are the circumstances for us talking after all these years, but I had actually been hoping our paths would cross." Kaira nods. "I don't have to tell you that the 4th Movement is transitioning—entering a new phase." Red is nodding like an idiot. "The Movement now has a center—something it never had before—and that center is ... well ... it's AAT. I think it's going to be the catalyst for real change." Te Wiata is surveying Kaira carefully for her reaction. "Don't get me wrong, all the bands are doing great work, but without coordination, we'll never get done what needs to get done."

"The Big One?" Kaira says with a wry smile.

Te Wiata smiles back. "That's all part of it, but there's a lot more, Kaira. And I want to bring you in. Ram's granddaughter needs to be part of it—in the heart of it."

Kaira doesn't respond.

"At the very least, I want to show you what we have here and then *you* decide."

Freya wants to do or say something that will help Kaira, but she doesn't know what that would be. She keeps her eyes locked on Kaira's. The chance to penetrate the Allfours is exactly why Freya is there but showing raw enthusiasm would be suspicious. On the other hand, the lady must not protest too much.

Te Wiata says, "Will you come here, Kaira, to let me show you what we're doing?" Kaira looks at him and then back at Freya, who musters a tight nod.

"Is that an invitation for all the Musketeers?"

"Of course it is," Te Wiata replies without hesitation. "The Musketeers have suffered enough fractures. Plus, I think if I have you all here, we'll have a better shot at tracking down your lost man. What do you say?" Kaira doesn't look at Red. She must know he'll be wagging his tail.

"Okay," she says.

TWENTY-FOUR

"Hi, Casy." Joad Bevan holds out his hand and pulls Dart up onto the pier.

"So this is an intervention."

"You look thin," Joad says.

"You look old. Where were you plucked from?"

"We're year-for-year since you left. But when your kid goes missing, that can cause some wear and tear."

Dart wants to tell his father that he's okay, but those words won't come out. Too much has happened. The engine of the small boat starts to rev and he turns to see it take off. "Where's Mom?"

"She's been detained, but she'll be here."

"She okay?"

"She works for HQ now. Pretty high-level job."

Dart shakes his head. "Wow. What an embarrassment I must be."

"We don't have a *Proud parents of an Allfour* bumper sticker if that's what you're asking."

Although he doesn't want to admit it, he had missed his father. The anomalies of temporal relocation had given him a father only a decade older than himself, so he had always seemed more like a big brother. And he had known Joad for only a couple of years before the Allfours had called. Dart surveys the panorama of forested peaks and the still lake they surround. "Where are we?"

"Beautiful, isn't it? Deep past. Safe place to be."

"Hidden in plain sight. That's pretty in-your-face."

"Yup. You're in Tomatotown. Tachyon interference shield around the entire periphery. Belts and suspenders."

"And that's why they had to accel me to the other side of the lake?"

"More to give you the view. C'mon, let's go inside." Joad begins to walk up the pier, but Dart stays put. Joad turns back, his smile fading. "This isn't an intervention, Casy. I don't think you need one. You know by now what the Allfours are about. You know the story they recruited with isn't the truth."

"Do I?"

"I think you do," Joad says as they walk up the pier.

"Everything I've done as an Allfour has been for the good—for the immediate good," Dart says. "And yes, I do still believe in the freedoms the Allfours defend." Had that sounded sophomoric? And why is he defending himself?

"I know that," Joad replies. He seems to sense that talking won't wait, and he nods towards a bench overlooking the lake. They sit.

From nowhere, a tsunami of emotion hits Dart and tears sheet over his eyes. Why does this happen? He hates that about himself. This time it's something about his father's smile, the warmth and familiarity of his voice. He's never seen a tear on Joad Bevan's face, nor any Musketeer's face for that matter. Who was it that said "the world is a tragedy for feeling people and a comedy for thinking people"? In him and Joad, the world had one of each. He quickly puts a hand to his eyes under the pretext of scratching an eyelid.

"But the 4th Movement is about more than that. You know that now, Casy. You know their theory of net moral neutrality is a pretext for doing anything they want to do, no matter how barbaric. And you know it's a bullshit theory based on cherry-picked data and half-assed analysis."

"There's a lot you think I know, Joad."

"There's a lot you *do* know, Casy."

A shrug is the most Dart's pride allows.

"And when you stood up and confronted Te Wiata, that's—"

"How do you know about that?"

Joad smiles at his son.

"TMA was there," Dart finally says. "So why didn't they swoop in and—"

"Swooping isn't the strategy, Casy."

"Do you know your TMA thugs short-charged my friend?"

Joad nods. "No one's happy about that. When TMA operatives have a mission, they get it done. Look, Casy, let's not go through the charade of my having to convince you of what the 4th Movement really is. It's a meltdown of reason run by psychopaths and nihilists who don't give a shit about the chaos and suffering they create. You've already figured that out for yourself. We could never have let you in here if we weren't already convinced of it, so let's not play-act my explaining it. The question is, what now?" Joad crosses his arms. "You have a choice, Casy."

Dart opens his mouth to reply when a shadow passes over them. "What the fuck?" It looks like a lone bird, long legs extended behind it, soaring high in the sky. He can't get a good sense of distance but it looks monstrous.

"Ha," Joad says nonchalantly. "You don't see them very often. And they don't seem interested in us. Nothing to worry about. Probably," Joad adds, grinning.

Dart smiles back and it feels good.

"We're preparing. We need to equal and exceed the resources the Allfours have. Where you are right now is the center of TMA Temporal Operations. TMATO. It's an aggregation of TMA's best and smartest, sourced from over a century of TMA operations. Yeah, the statue's a joke but there's not much else funny about the situation we're in. The

Allfours have a natural advantage and it's the second law of thermodynamics—the law of increasing entropy. It's a lot easier to break things than to put them back together."

Dart hadn't noticed the change when it happened, but he now feels calm, and the shivering has stopped. He looks back over his shoulder at the complex behind him. "And what goes on in the big Tomato?"

"We'll get to all of that." Joad stands but Dart remains seated.

"Let's get to it now," Dart says. Joad looks at his son for a moment and then sits back down.

"I'd forgotten what an irritating little shit you can be. Okay. Three major missions are going on. One: understand and maybe cross the tachyon horizon. Answer the question of why there seems to be a brick wall for tachyons at the end of the twenty-first century. Is it a natural barrier? Seems unlikely. And if it's human-made, which humans made it? We know TMA doesn't have the technology. We can create a shield that temporarily protects a chunk of space, but this shield, whatever it is, seems to be a global barrier in time. There's no getting through it for tachyons in either direction. And whoever figures out how to cross that horizon is going to have access to some pretty advanced technologies—at least that's what we assume. If that *whoever* turns out to be the Movement, then ...

"Two: Predictive analytics of temporal edits; how to forecast the impact on the timeline. We need to be able to predict how our little capers in history are going to change things, or more to the point for TMA, how they might remedy things."

"And I can take a guess at Mission Three," Dart says. Joad indicates *go for it*.

"The Big One."

Joad leans forward and studies Dart's face. "And what is the Big One?"

"I was about to ask *you*," Dart says. He had sat through a lecture from Te Wiata on what the Big One *isn't* which left everyone guessing what it *is*. Joad waits as if unsure whether Dart has said all he intends to. After a long pause, Dart asks, "So what is Mission Three?"

"Oh, it's pretty straightforward. Eliminate Barry Te Wiata."

TWENTY-FIVE

The farmhouse kitchen is there and then it isn't. Having jabbed in encrypted spacetime coordinates, 1964 rural England is a thing of the past, or maybe the future, and the place that now surrounds Freya is dark and cold. It looks like the interior of a cave. *Now, this is unexpected.* Adrenaline floods her. *Reverse, reverse.* Freya had been taught how to return instantly to the place of departure, but the accelerator isn't responding. She's prodding a dead screen. The cave is featureless but for the harsh fluorescent light hanging from the low ceiling and a large metal plate in the wall she takes to be a door. She pushes her shoulder against the metal, but there's no give. She has accelerated herself right into a jail cell.

"Hey," she shouts. The air is damp. "Hey," this time louder.

The door slides open and Red bursts in, beaming. "What the hell is all the fuss, Slayer? You're gonna get us thrown out."

She grabs Red by the arm. "What the fuck is happening here? Why were we separated?"

"Just calm down, will you?" Freya dislikes violence, but when it's called for ...

Red is dumb enough to still be smiling. "Hey, just listen to me," he says, holding up his palms in self-defense. "They had good reasons."

"What reasons?"

"I've been here a couple days and I'd meant to be here when you arrived. Sorry."

"You acceled to two days earlier?"

"Yes, they needed to brief me."

"Brief *you*? On what?"

"We're already pulled into their operations, Slayer. And we have our first mission. How cool is that? Turns out the Musketeers' field experience is more than most of the Movement's chair meat have."

Freya shakes her head in bewilderment. "What mission? Where's Kaira?"

"Kaira's with Te Wiata. They want to catch up."

"No, the deal was we stay together. Where is she?" Freya takes a deep breath and blows it out. She needs to keep it together. "Are we in a friggin' cave?"

"The whole place is cut into rock. One big-ass grotto. Pretty amazing."

Has Red's enthusiasm always felt this infantile? She turns to him and says, "My accelerator stopped working."

"Whole place is inside a tachyon interference shield. They deactivate it only for transmissions." The tinge of condescension in Red's smile is right on the boundary of what Freya will allow herself to tolerate. "You okay now?"

"So we're going to see Te Wiata?"

"No need. We have the mission details. Here." Red removes a handgun from the back of his belt and thrusts the grip towards Freya.

"Shit, no."

He forces it into Freya's hand and takes a second gun from his belt. "No big deal."

"How many do you have back there?"

Red ignores the question. "You take off the safety, grip the rack here, pull it back hard, and you're ready to shoot."

Freya steps back from Red. "No. Shoot what?"

"Shoot people who are a problem."

"You'd better start making sense, Red, because right now, *you're* the problem."

"Just relax, will you?"

Freya stares at the gun in her hand. "And that was my training?"

"You're going to fire a gun, not remove a tumor," Red says, tucking his gun back into his belt. "This is a mission from Te Wiata himself. That puts us in the inner sanctum. Get excited, Slayer."

Freya looks into Red's big, banal eyes. What the hell had she done? What course of events had brought her to this point? She couldn't relate to the Freya who had done those things—the Freya who had been attracted to him because he was handsome and borderline funny. Now, the perceptions of *that* Freya are unfathomable. In front of her is a pathetic little fucker, excited by the idea that someone he thinks is important thinks that *he's* important.

Jenn will keep her sane—thinking about the plan. That's why she's here, wherever *here* is. This is what will stop her using her new pistol right there and then.

Red grabs Freya's hand and holds a small, disk-shaped device up to her accelerator. "You're set."

"Where are we going?" she asks.

"Vancouver, British Columbia. 1918."

"Why Van—"

"—couver?" Freya is bathed in sunlight and she shuts her eyes. It takes her body a few moments to register the warmth and the smell of smoke in the air. She opens her eyes to see a large vehicle passing by that looks like a box on wheels. Out of the windows, some passengers are staring at her, open-mouthed. They must have seen her pop in. She looks up the sidewalk and some of the pedestrians are frozen in their tracks with others walking around them.

Directly in front of them is a large building.

Reid's Fine Meats.

"This is it," Red says.

Freya looks down. "Look at how we're dressed."

"Don't worry about that, Slayer. We won't be here long enough for it to matter. Come on." Next to the butcher shop facade there's a narrow recess in the wall, and a door at the back of it. Red walks up to the door, removing the pistol from his belt as he beckons Freya to follow him through to the lobby of a tenement. They step into an aroma of spicy food and as Freya's stomach begins to rumble, she realizes that she hasn't eaten in a long while. "Okay, just listen to me. We're going up two flights of stairs and we're going into one of these slums. Inside there'll be a bunch of girls. Shoot them."

It takes a second for Freya to understand what she had heard. She grabs Red's shoulder. "Shoot them? What—"

"In fact, just shoot anyone in there to be safe. Got it?"

"No, I don't *got it*."

"You're an Allfour now, Slayer. Remember ... net moral neutrality. The little shits will probably produce some genocidal maniac at some point in the timeline, so we're dealing with it now. Probably saving millions of lives. Ready?"

Her hunger is replaced by the urge to vomit. How far does she take this to stay embedded? Not waiting for her answer, Red moves towards the staircase. She hesitates, then follows. Halfway up the second flight of stairs, an old Indian man begins to say something to Red, which earns him a blow from the side of Red's pistol, and Freya hears a crunch before the old man tumbles down the steps towards her. Suddenly, she doesn't recognize herself. She's holding a semi-automatic pistol and is actually contemplating using it on a man she has been screwing for a year. It'd be easy, so easy. Maybe just wound him. She steps over the old man who is still breathing, to her relief.

As she catches up with Red he's already knocking on an

apartment door. It's a light, friendly knock that says *I hope I'm not bothering you.* A moment passes before the door is cracked ajar and Red kicks it wide open. He gives Freya a horrendous grin and flicks his head for her to follow. She steps over a woman who's wrapped in a white shawl, crying out something in a language she doesn't understand. In the small living area, they find a young girl in a white sari. She backs away from them and Red, seemingly without deliberation, lifts his gun and shoots her in the head. Freya gasps, watching in slow motion as the girl tumbles backwards onto a small table, too light to knock it over, and just lies across it, staring up blankly.

Red takes stock of the room. There are two doors: one open, one closed. He points his gun at the closed door. "Take out whoever's in there," he says, then walks towards the open door. Freya can see movement through the doorway. She turns away before the gunfire begins. She expects there to be screams and sounds of panic but there are none—only rapid gunfire.

Shaking, she opens her assigned door and cowering in the corner is a woman draped over a small child. The woman looks up at Freya with wild eyes. The gunfire stops and Red's footsteps echo through the space. She slams the door closed. "No one," she says to him. "It's empty."

Red casually turns to the old lady crumpled by the shattered front door, and is about to turn back to Freya when, as an afterthought, he fires two shots into the woman. Freya can't catch her breath. "Okay. We're done," he says.

Freya peers through the open door behind Red. There's a shattered window and blood on the floor, but she can't make out anything else. "Accelerator," Red barks. Freya lifts her hand, hoping to god that Jenn's accelerator is doing its job. He holds his programmer close to it and the scene of the massacre vanishes.

TWENTY-SIX

She's back in the cave and the man looking at her is a goblin. Wire-framed glasses, shiny pate, long unkempt sideburns. On tiptoes he might reach her navel. The woman standing next to the goblin is a contrast in scale.

The goblin holds out his hands. "Give," he snaps.

Freya doesn't know what this means until Red hands over his pistol. She does the same.

The goblin hands the guns to the woman. "Come." He turns and walks briskly out of the room. Freya and Red exchange a glance, not sure what to do. The woman impatiently nods them ahead.

They navigate narrow passages of pale rock with low-hanging fluorescent lights running overhead. The passages are curved, continually concealing what's ahead, which generally turns out to be more curving passages. They pass two women coming in the other direction who avoid eye contact but back up against the wall to allow the goblin and the rest of them through. Eventually, they reach a metal door in the rock wall that slides open to reveal the interior of an elevator.

Freya's stomach is left behind as the elevator plummets. In the cramped space she feels the goblin's eyes on the back of her neck and the woman's ass on her stomach. The elevator's deceleration is severe. Why does such a short journey require the elevator to reach such speed? It had been only a slight improvement on simply falling.

The door opens and they step into a space that's not much larger than the elevator. Another metal door in the rock wall opposite opens, and the laconic goblin instructs them to enter.

The harsh fluorescent lighting of the corridor is replaced by the soft light of a table lamp on a dark oak desk. This cave appears to be an office, and as Freya's eyes adapt, she sees Barry Te Wiata half in shadow behind the desk. He's not wearing the friendly, smiling face he had on the tackynet call, and this is not the homely kitchen that had been his backdrop. Behind him are two men. One, like Te Wiata, has a shaven head, but this guy is pale-skinned and wiry with islands of acne across his face. He's tall, his head almost touching the cave top, and his tiny rat eyes and pinched mouth somehow convey the spirit of casual violence. But it's the other man who'd win the prize for absurd incongruity—white shirt, red tie and jacket, like a banker. Both men are staring at Red.

"How did it go?" Te Wiata says softly without looking up.

"Mission accomplished," Red says, beaming.

"Was it? Good." There's a silence and Red glances at Freya. "Tell me."

"Eliminated everyone in the apartment." Red turns back to Freya for confirmation, but she can barely muster a nod.

"Tell me who you eliminated."

Freya has a sense that things are not going well.

"Every woman and girl in there."

Te Wiata stands and walks slowly around his desk until he's toe to toe with Red. He towers over him. "And how many was that?"

"Not sure, but everyone is dead. I'm sure about that."

"Are you?" Te Wiata's face is now inches from Red's.

"Well, good." Then he smiles. "You know, anyone who says they really understand temporal logic is too dumb to know they don't. But there are some things we can be sure we *do* know." Te Wiata jabs his finger in Red's chest in rhythm with these last few words. "When you edit events, the timeline transitions, shifts, snaps. We get a new timeline. Sure, we all know there's some elasticity that seems to want to heal the effects of any edit, but there's always some evidence of it to us tuskers, right?"

This is theater—a villain prolonging the moment. Yet, it's having the desired effect if that's to scare her. What's unnerving is that she's used to hearing such words and ideas in a safe and familiar environment. Surrounded by people like her. It's as if such knowledge should create refinement, civility, and values she shares. Yet here's this gangster speaking the words, barely holding back something dangerous and violent.

"But you know," Te Wiata continues, "sometimes you can be absolutely sure of the effects an edit will have. And it happens that I have a litmus test of whether or not you were successful." She can hear her heart pounding in her ears. "You see, you were supposed to kill every female member of the Agarwal family in that apartment. You know why?" Red looks too terrified to risk an answer. "Because one of those women was going to give birth to a fine and important chap called Ramesh Prasad." Freya can't suppress a gasp. "And a few meters from here is my litmus test, you see. Can you guess what it is?" Te Wiata drops his ham shank hand onto Red's shoulder, causing his knees to buckle.

"Kaira?" Red whispers.

Te Wiata nods. "Yes, temporal logic can be a mystery, but we do know that granddaughters don't survive failure to be born. So do you want to know how she is?" Red's nod is barely perceptible. "She's well, thank you. Very well, indeed."

The rat-eyed crony is still glaring at Red, but the banker

is looking at the ground, as if any eye-to-eye contact would be unwise.

"That's both good news and bad. Good because I love her like family. Bad because it means you've failed me."

"We killed them all." Red looks to Freya in a plea for confirmation. "Every ... everyone—"

"Don't stutter, Athos." Te Wiata walks back behind his desk and sits. "Like I said, temporal logic is a strange thing. Even the greatest minds don't understand it, let alone imbeciles."

Te Wiata turns his big, shiny face on Freya for the first time. He stares. Freya knows she's supposed to be terrified, so she returns his stare. She'd crossed paths with a lot of bullies in her time. You don't get to avoid them when you're a woman—a black woman. And she'd dealt with them all. But this creature is different. Before, there had been no real threat of violence, at least none that she couldn't have dealt with head-on. But this one had just told her he'd ordered killings that should have vanished someone he considers family. So her first reaction is contained by second thoughts, and *fuck you, asshole* is not what she says.

TWENTY-SEVEN

Assertive door-knocking is something Dart had never appreciated, and he's especially in no mood for it after a sleepless night of reconstructing Porthos's fate. And he needs Kaira. His side seems cold, raw, and exposed without her there next to him. It's strange how quickly you become only half of something.

He gets out of bed and crosses the small living space. He opens the door and it's a face he recognizes: the woman who had ferried him across the lake, and she's still smiling.

"C'mon, buckeroo. I'm going to give you a bit of a tour."

"You're a tour guide now?"

"Yeah, c'mon."

"I thought you were the skipper of the ferry."

"That's not a full-time job. I do a lot of things around here." Her eyes are that palest of blues, where you could easily believe she's a visitor from a neighboring planet. He realizes he's staring, and quickly affects to look behind him to make sure the apartment is as it should be before leaving.

They set off in a golf cart, a refreshing chill in the air, towards the main building with its dais-mounted tomato. People walking in twos and threes stand aside for the silent cart to pass. Some know his chauffeur and wave.

"How many people are here?" Dart asks.

"Not authorized to answer that," she says in a musical tone, as if he had asked the same question a hundred times before.

"Are you authorized to tell me your name?"

"Max."

"I'm Dart."

"Dart! Okay, Dart," she says, as if she'll settle for that. She drives past the glass building towards one of the concrete structures. It's a huge cube of maybe fifty yards with only a single door visible. "That's the detection facility. Below us there's a five-hundred-acre tachyon detection array."

"And what are you looking for?"

She doesn't answer, and they drive to the next structure, which is another concrete cube about half the size of the first. "And that's where we house the main accelerator for bulk transport."

"That's how you got all this here? What's its volumetric rate?" Again, no response. "As tour guides go, you're not big on answers, are you?"

"Oh, Darty."

Dart is taken off guard. Only Kaira had ever called him *Darty*, and he has a pang of guilt for not having thought about her for the past few minutes. Max is obviously one of those people who assumes instant familiarity. "I'm not actually a scientist. One of the few here who isn't." There's something unsettling about that. "But you're the director's kid. Ask *him* your questions." Dart's surprise must have shown. "Joad's the Tomato king. He didn't tell you?"

Dart shakes his head. Holy shit. What an embarrassment he must be. "So what's a regular human doing here? Where were you plucked from?"

"Los Angeles, 1964."

"1964? There was no TMA then. How can you have been recruited from 1964?"

"I'm a natural tusker. Got the weird chemical cocktail in

me. Before the tusker serum, that was quite a commodity to have, you know. They recruited a few of us—the only ones who could detect a timeline shift. Useful to know, right? Of course, they don't really need us anymore, but I have my uses."

The main building of blue-tinted glass is the next stop and Dart gets a walking tour. It couldn't be more different from the dank, claustrophobic spaces TMA usually occupies. The lobby is bathed in natural light with multiple staircases ascending to a mezzanine. Someone shouts *hi* down to Max and she waves back. Dart is toured past sunlit offices, through large open spaces containing big-ticket electromagnets and nuclear magnetic resonance spectrometers, to lab benches covered in loose electronic components, then wet labs with fume hoods and chemicals bubbling through tubes from flask to flask. He's missed the science, he realizes—the research.

In the final stop, they look down from a balcony onto a complex of quantum computing machinery, with people walking around and between them like mice in a maze. This technology postdates the point in the timeline from which he had plucked himself. He asks no questions.

It's a large cafeteria, and all the tables are unoccupied except for one, which is full. In the center, like the Messiah at the last supper, is Dart's father. Most of the twenty-some others at the table are looking at Joad, who must be saying something funny. Although, in Dart's experience, when you're the boss, the threshold for funny can be low. Joad sees Dart and Max enter and waves them over. Two of Joad's audience reluctantly make space on either side of him.

Dart and Max are immediately drawn into a series of shifting conversations: the evolution of swear words over the twentieth and twenty-first centuries, the progression of music in a Schoenberg-free timeline, and the ability to quantize a tachyon field near the event horizon of a black hole. These people obviously love Joad, and he looks like he loves them loving him.

"What's it like to have a father who won the revolutionary war for the Americans?" asks a toady young guy with greasy shoulder-length hair. He looks at his colleagues for affirmation of his wit.

"You know better than that, George," Joad says.

The conversation continues as the audience thins until finally Dart and Joad are alone.

"I'm glad you enjoyed the tour. No one who spends time with Max feels down at the end of it. You needed that."

"Yeah, she is interesting," Dart says. Joad nods, and then his smile fades. It's a look Dart remembers as the precursor to some tough love.

"They have Kaira," Joad says. "Te Wiata has her."

"What do you mean, *has* her?" Dart's stomach tightens.

"He's been collecting Allfours, and some go more voluntarily than others. He's centralizing his operations."

"And she's not free to leave?"

"As far as we can tell, once they're in there, their accelerators are controlled centrally. And we're assuming they're inside a pretty solid tachyon interference shield. No one in or out without Te Wiata's say so."

"So what are we going to do?"

"We can try and get her out, Casy. Better still, we can try and get them all out. Even a bunch of crazy maverick Allfours is less of a threat than some coordinated effort under Te Wiata."

"Crazy like I am, you mean?"

"Crazy like you *were*, Casy."

"And a coordinated effort to do what? How do we get her out?"

Joad shakes his head, then says, "We have someone embedded. She was wearing one of our accelerators when she acceled to Te Wiata's base, and it's been transmitting a tachyon-encoded data stream back to us. In principle, we can know where she was acceled to, and so where Te Wiata is holed up."

"In principle?"

"There's a bit of a hurdle. They programmed her accelerator with encrypted data, and that's what was sent to us. The better news is that we have a good shot at decrypting it."

Dart pushes his chair back from the table, causing a shriek to echo through the empty cafeteria. He takes a few deep, shaky breaths. He has to keep it together, especially in front of Joad. "So we can decrypt the accelerator data?"

"It's a challenge, for sure. It's quantum-encrypted. But with any decryption, it's always just a matter of time. With conventional quantum computing, we figure it'd take more than 10,000 years to decrypt." Dart waits attentively for the *but*. "But time is something we know a little about. We're working on a method we call tachyonic decryption. Ten thousand years doesn't sound so bad when you can relay and iterate data up and down the timeline." Dart looks blankly at his father. "The guy who's developing it is the one who was just up my ass."

"Which one? Looks like you have a lot of people up there."

"I know. With that many scientists up there I'll never need a colonoscopy. But George is the one."

Dart sits back in his chair and tries to slowly exhale his tension. He's not happy with the idea that rescuing Kaira calls for a computing breakthrough.

"By the way," Joad says, "a mission our mole had been sent on was to eliminate Prasad. And they were trying to do it in a real Allfours kind of way. They wanted to take out his mother ... as a child."

Dart blinks in surprise. "What? Why would Te Wiata want to cut off Prasad? He made Te Wiata."

"That's true, but you have to think like Te Wiata. You'd asked me if I knew what the Big One is. I don't but let me ask you this. If you were a psychopathic narcissist, what sort of things might the Big One be to you?

"It'd be something about *him*."

"Yeah, it'd be all about Barry Te Wiata. Everyone assumed it was something big, like sending the entire human race down a different path because that sounds as big as it can get, but for Te Wiata it can get bigger. It can be about Barry Te Wiata. I think he believes that if Prasad were eliminated from the timeline, it'd be him who'd be the father of tackychemistry, the father of time travel."

"But that's crazy. A world without Prasad could go in a billion different directions. Te Wiata wouldn't just step into the job. Without Prasad, Te Wiata could be in Tauranga teaching middle school physics."

"I don't think he sees it that way. I think it's obvious to him that he'd fill the Prasad gap. And he probably has shit analytics that some poor bastards produced with a view to surviving."

Dart looks out through the large wall windows at the deep blue sky. "So Kaira will be pretty fucking useful to him," he says.

"To say the least."

TWENTY-EIGHT

"Sorry to keep you waiting," the Allfour operative says to Freya without looking at her. His wire-framed spectacles, black frock coat, bright-red waistcoat, and black doorknocker beard make him look like he's straight off a nineteenth-century Christmas card. She had noticed that some Allfours operatives tend to take a fancy to one of the eras they have visited, then start to get eccentric about it. The walls of the small room are lined with hundreds of wrist accelerators hanging from hooks.

"Size?" he asks Freya. "Just kidding. I say that to everyone. One size fits all. C'mon, take that one off." *Oh shit.* This means she won't be going home soon, wherever home might be. "We're going to fix you up with a much better model. What is that? *Circa* early twenty-first? A bit old-fashioned for here."

This guy knows his accelerators. It doesn't escape Freya that a man wearing a frock coat is declaring her accelerator old-fashioned.

"Here you go." He puts the accelerator on Freya's left wrist and tightens it until it clicks. Her pulse races.

"Have you locked that on me?"

"Oh yes," he replies. "For your own safety. No one

wants to be stranded out there without their accelerator, do they? And it's centrally programmed for whatever mission you're being sent on—its actuation synchronized with the shield. I think you'll like it."

"So I can't program it myself?"

"Why would you need to?" He throws her old accelerator into a drawer that seals itself. "You're done," he says with a fatherly smile. "Off with you."

Red is waiting for her in the corridor.

"I just got tagged by Charles friggin' Dickens," Freya hisses. Red grabs her roughly by the arm and Freya pulls back. "What the hell?"

He lets go and walks off. Freya follows and hears him muttering to himself. "What's going on, Red?"

He stops. "You know, you could have supported me in there instead of just looking at me like a fucking fish."

"How?"

"By telling Te Wiata we killed everyone in that apartment. Every one of them."

"Maybe Prasad's mother wasn't in there."

"Do you think?" he replies with savage irony. Red prods his own temple hard and says, "Is that what thinking it through tells you?"

Freya hasn't seen Red angry before, and it's more pathetic than scary. It's obvious that this little shit had been working with Te Wiata long before they had acceled out of the farmhouse, and now the man whose ass he had been enthusiastically climbing up thinks he's an imbecile.

They walk in silence until the corridor opens onto a balcony. It overlooks a huge cavern. The ceiling of rock formations must be a hundred feet high, with fluorescent lights and a network of ventilation conduits suspended from it. The cave floor, which is the area of a football field, probably more, is covered with tents and cots, groups of Allfours milling around between them. The sound of a hundred conversations echoes throughout this dizzying natural cathedral, and Freya grabs the balcony railing for balance. Around the cave are other balconies from which people are looking down onto the camp. There's a staircase to the camp floor, and Red begins to descend it. Freya follows, grabbing the handrail tightly.

"What is this?" she asks.

"The dormitory," Red replies curtly.

"So do you think your friend Dart is somewhere down there?" she says to Red's back.

"No. Te Wiata says they didn't take him and that's good enough for me. And right now I'm in no mood to care." They reach the ground and begin navigating the people and tents. It reminds Freya of rock festivals she'd seen on documentaries, but without the music. Red stops at a bed that's positioned amidst a clutch of small tents. "This is ours," he says. Freya stares at it. "I can put up a tent if you're shy," he says.

"Put up a tent," she says, and he walks off without replying.

Freya sits on the bed. It would have been so easy to say *no* to Jenn. So easy. She'd given her a hundred opportunities to say *no*. And if Freya had had a clue what she was signing up for, it would have been a complete and utter no-brainer. Wouldn't it? Maybe not. She takes in a deep breath and whistles it out to steady herself. No one seems to notice her. She's just a woman sitting on a bed in a cave. All these people look like typical TMAers in jeans, T-shirts or plaid, with a few wearing ludicrous outfits from various eras.

The flap of a small green tent in front of her opens and a woman ducks out. She flashes a smile at Freya, yawns, and stretches her arms. She has short, gray hair and Freya places her in her fifties. She doesn't mean to, but something makes her stare at the woman. She's sure she knows her from somewhere. The woman notices Freya and stares back. Realization crosses the woman's face.

"I know you," she says.

Freya blinks and the reality of time travel suddenly hits her like a train. "Yes," Freya says. "You're Sarah. Sarah Bari

... Freya Beaufort."

"Freya Beaufort," the woman echoes. "Oh, wow." They stare at each other, smiling. "And here you are. You joined up, and by the look of you, not long after I last saw you." Sarah's face is finely lined, and her eyes are red and watery, but Freya can still see in her the dryad she'd known. Sure, time travel is big-concept stuff and the math of it is intriguing, but it's the human dimension that's knocking Freya backwards. This makes it all real, and it's madness.

"Yup, I joined up. And you did, too?"

"Long after you left, but yes."

"How long have you been an Allfour?"

"Ten years. A year here," Sarah says.

Freya looks up at the observation balconies. Some guy dressed like a lumberjack is watching her. She turns back to Sarah. "A year here? Do you know where *here* is?"

Sarah shakes her head.

"A year seems like a long time to live in a ... cave. You okay with that?"

Sarah looks at Freya with curiosity more than suspicion. "It's not a Hawaiian vacation, but it's all for the cause, right?"

Freya nods. What irony, that an organization with the sacred cause of freedom of movement has its followers locked up in a cave. They look at each other awkwardly. It seems there should be a lot to talk about, but Freya can't think of anything to say. The Sarah she remembers was effervescent and excited by just about everything. Freya had only tolerated that, but it was better than this—a wound-down Sarah.

"Talk later," Sarah says. "I need to ..." She points somewhere and walks off.

Freya is awoken by the kerfuffle. She's fully dressed and lying next to Red on a bed, exposed for all to see. He hadn't been able to get his hands on a tent, although she suspects he was too peeved with her to put much effort into it. She's hearing a man's voice and he's protesting something. Then there are other men's voices, calmer but just as loud. In the dimmed light she can't make out what's going on, although she glimpses between tents what looks like someone being frog-marched away.

No one seems to be coming out of their tents, and Red doesn't stir. Maybe they're all used to it—the visits in the night. Red's mouth is open and he's drooling onto his pillow. Freya watches him breathe. She had always prided herself on never hating anyone, because the haters she'd known had always been small, insecure, talentless people. Now she needs to rethink that because she definitely hates Red.

TWENTY-NINE

Surrounded by such genius and innovation, Dart knows he should be diving into new ideas, exploring mind-stretching science, and learning about technologies that verge on the miraculous; but instead, his days are spent gazing into the electric blue sky. One of the large flying creatures passes over occasionally, its shadow racing across the still lake. They are always alone, never in flocks. A flock of them would turn day into night. He still can't make out what exactly they are: maybe reptiles, maybe just damn big birds. Whichever it is, this place must be one hell of a jog into the past—a lot further than he's gone before.

He focuses on trying to reason away his darkest fears. *Te Wiata wouldn't harm Kaira. Why would he? He needs her intact. Kill off Prasad and the timeline will snap to one in which Kaira just doesn't exist.* Unfathomably, no one—at least no one in the Movement—seems to think of that sort of thing as doing harm anymore. Preventing a life, preventing a billion lives. That's insanity—even to someone who had been brought up with this new science and its ludicrous logic.

And if Te Wiata really had any confidence in the crazy forecast that he would end up filling the Prasad gap, then why would he need Kaira? If the mad universe shoves him into the Prasad-shaped hole, surely he'd know that pretty damn fast. But Dart realizes he's trying to ascribe a sense of reason to a straight-up lunatic. His stomach is in knots. He can't remember the last time it wasn't, but these knots are tighter, bigger, heavier.

Joad places a hand on Dart's shoulder, startling him out of his thoughts. "What're you seeing out there?" Joad asks. Dart shrugs. "Those flyers are big bastards aren't they?" Dart nods.

"You always were a talker, Casy." Joad squeezes his son's shoulder. "The good news is, we think we're nearly there on the accelerator decryption. We've been shunting data and solutions up and down the timeline and—"

"So where is she?"

"Not yet. Soon."

"How soon?"

Joad smiles at his son. "I want to show you something."

They ascend the incline in single file: Max, then Dart, then Joad bringing up the rear. It's not so much a path, more ground worn bare by foot traffic. The forest on the slope is dense with only a few yards of visibility.

"Any animals to worry about?" Dart asks, scanning the trees and shrubs.

"No," Joad replies. "This is a small island with a big lake in the middle and we've scouted it pretty well. No animals apart from benign insects and the giant flyers that pass over."

"Then why is she carrying a big game rifle?" Dart asks.

"Precaution."

Dart looks up at Max who's snapping off twigs to clear the path. "Exactly what is her job description?"

After thirty minutes of ascent, more sky becomes visible as they come nearer to cresting the hill. Max waves them forward, and as they catch up, what comes into view is a sparkling ocean under a cloudless, sapphire sky. Looking down the treeless slope on the far side of the hilltop, Dart sees at the bottom a rigid frame metal building enclosed by a high-wire fence.

"Welcome to Tomato West," Max says.

"Not too impressive to look at compared to Tomatotown," Joad says, "but I think what's in there might interest you."

They descend the slope along the well-worn path that now cuts through shrubs and thicket. There's a gate in the fence, and next to it, a guardhouse out of which steps a guy carrying a machine gun. Max shouts something to him Dart can't make out and the guard smiles as he slings the weapon over his shoulder.

"Hello, Dr. Bevan," he calls. Two more guards step out and greet Dart's father as *Sir*. What can be in such need of guarding? This whole place is so unfindable that they're comfortable housing TMA operations in a shining city on a lake, yet there's something here they need to guard?

One of the guards clips a *Visitor* credential onto each of them, and they enter the fenced area in turn through a full-height turnstile, which is equipped with an ultrafrequency weapons detector. It's just a few paces to the building's entrance, little more than a hinged flap cut out of the metal wall.

The interior has none of the flash of the main Tomato building. They walk along hospital-green corridors, passing a few offices with internal glass windows. This looks more like the TMA he remembers. Max leads them through a door, and the space that opens up before them contains a maze of randomly distributed servers, whiteboards, and work benches strewn with hardware. People are sitting at terminals, or tinkering with electronic components, or just chatting. Some look up as Joad's team enters, but their interest is quickly lost.

"Looks a little more mainstream TMA than the Tomato setup, doesn't it?" Max says.

"What's going on here?" Dart asks his father.

"R&D."

Two men with their backs to them are scribbling formulas on a whiteboard. Dart squints to see if he can make anything of what they're writing, but it just looks like generic quantum field theory punctuated with Feynman diagrams. "So why do you have this setup?" Dart asks.

Then the two men turn. The older one is short and maybe Indian, the other much taller and younger. The Indian guy looks ... Dart catches his breath.

He turns to his father who's grinning. "Is that ...?

Joad nods. "It is. That's Ram Prasad."

Max's attention is entirely on the two men. The younger man has a thick mop of black hair and is looking at Max like they know each other. He seems familiar, and Dart thinks he's on the verge of placing him when Joad adds, "Oh, and that's Barry Te Wiata."

Max approaches him and Te Wiata stoops to place a quick kiss on her cheek.

"What?"

"Oh yes," Joad says. He and Max are ... a thing." Prasad had already turned back to the whiteboard, continuing his scribbling as if nothing shiveringly ludicrous had just happened. Te Wiata and Max are sharing a joke.

"What the fuck?" is the best question Dart can come up with.

"What indeed," his father replies. Dart looks at the insane and appalling scene in front of him.

"I'm sure you've already thought of this," Dart says, "but if a Tomato mission is to eliminate Te Wiata, then ..." Joad doesn't answer. "Where are they plucked from?"

"1988. A golden year for Prasad—just formulating the principles of tackychemistry, of time travel."

"And he's doing it here? With Barry Te Wiata?"

"A safe place for them."

"Safe? It shouldn't be safe for Te Wiata. Why not make it very fucking unsafe for Te Wiata?"

"You mean kill him? We're not Allfours, Casy. The Te

Wiata over there is innocent. And besides, we can't tell how vital his role was ... is. We don't want to upset the apple cart."

Dart feels dizzy just coming up with questions, let alone dealing with the answers. "So they're creating tackychemistry right here. Right here in ... Tomato West?" Dart tries to organize a hundred thoughts into one coherent set. "But they're surrounded by people versed in tackychemistry. Experts. That's like Edison working on the first electric bulb and doing it under a high-wattage lamp."

"Ha. I think you're asking about causal loops. That's what the first question usually is. No good answers yet but we have an entire team working on causal topology—connectivities of cause and effect. True enough, conventional physics has no place for them, but now we have no place for conventional physics. It seems causal loops can and do happen." He pauses to let that sink in. But we are trying to keep these two isolated from the full Tomato team. Even I don't communicate with them. I just look from afar. There are rules about what Prasad and Te Wiata can be told, what resources they can access, and everyone in this facility knows those rules. The idea is to accelerate their work, not just hand it to them on a platter."

"Seems like a subtle distinction to me." Dart watches them: Te Wiata deciphering Prasad's whiteboard scribblings and Max staring lovingly at Te Wiata. He wonders if he'll ever again get through just one hour without receiving a monumental shock. "No. This doesn't make sense."

"It is difficult. My temporal logicians have a way of looking at it. They say our modes of thought are constrained by having seen the world through the lens of the old physics and conventional logic. That our intuition about the way the world works and what makes sense won't just change in a generation. We shouldn't expect our intuition to keep pace with the science."

As he watches a young, innocent Te Wiata, Dart's thoughts switch to Kaira. "What happened to him? What changed?"

Joad shrugs. "Don't know but being number two can take its toll in the end. And nothing warrants revenge like kindness."

THIRTY

It's not half bad for food that had been spit from a vending machine, although Freya usually prefers something requiring teeth. The lighting had been dimmed by a few Watts, so this was to be considered nighttime. There's a smattering of people in the mess hall, yet another cavern, with some sitting alone staring into their bowls and others in small groups talking quietly. It's less capacious than the dormitory and contains long dining tables with vending machines lining the walls. She imagines the mush she's eating being acceled in bulk to the base and then extruded into various shapes that suggest *food*.

Freya grasps the accelerator that has been locked to her wrist. It has no control screen, just a single button, the purpose of which had not been explained. She has lost track of time with nothing like a real cycle of light and dark to guide her, but guesses she's been living this troglodytic life for about a week. Sarah has been her main company. Red disappears each day and shares nothing when he returns. They sleep together under a tent that Red erected around their cot but few words are exchanged, and Red couldn't get it up to save his life. That was at least one bright note.

Freya had spent the day looking for Dart, not so much

driven by excitement to find him but for respite from the boredom. The only reprieve from the tedium had been the scuffles that broke out intermittently between Allfours. It had amused Freya that they fought exactly as you'd expect PhD physicists to fight. At least she'd have no trouble dealing with any hostility, having spent a year kicking the asses of drunken nerds and jocks alike. And then between the scuffles there had been the laughing, singing, and even dancing. Allfours have a certain schizophrenia about their circumstances.

There were maybe three hundred or so Allfours holed up there—a lot more than she'd seen in that Glasgow lecture theater. Was TMA even aware of the size of Te Wiata's army? Maybe the Glasgow Allfours were just the ones who hadn't yet been lured here.

Lost in thought, she didn't see Red approach her table. He sits across from her. "We have a mission," he says.

Freya locks eyes with him. He had gotten steadily less angry with her over the past few days and now looks more excited than livid. She wasn't sure which she preferred.

"They've tracked down an ancestor. A Prasad ancestor. We've been picked to eliminate him."

Freya spoons more formless mush food into her mouth. "They're just determined to vanish Kaira, aren't they?" she says after choking down the mouthful.

"They don't give a crap about Kaira," he replies.

Had Red always been this stupid? What's horrifying is that this is someone who'd talked her into bed and into a year-long relationship. Sure, Jenn had eventually encouraged it, but at first it had all been Freya's doing. Hell, how lonely could she have been? What she'd now give to unfuck this sad imbecile and to have gotten a pound dog instead.

"Who's this ancestor?"

"A soldier in the Battle of Hydaspes. We have exact coords."

"Never heard of it. And *battle* sounds dangerous."

"It was a battle between Alexander's army and the Indian king, Porus."

"Alexander ...?"

"The Great."

Freya throws down her spoon, its clatter drawing attention from a young, ginger-haired guy at a nearby table. "Fuck you." Red is dumb enough to be surprised. "That was like, what?—two-and-a-half thousand years ago?"

"326 BCE." Freya had forgotten about Red's idiotic party trick, maybe because she had associated it with someone she liked.

"It's a suicide mission," she says. "It's designed as a suicide mission. Can't you see that? Putting us in the middle of a battle? And how could they have traced Prasad's ancestry back that far?"

"They have the analytics to do it."

"Bullshit. And why go back that far, anyway? It makes no sense. They just want to kill us off. It's Kaira that Te Wiata wanted, not us."

"No," Red says with banal sincerity. "He's giving us a chance to redeem ourselves after the Vancouver fiasco."

"He's giving us a chance to kill ourselves, Red." Freya throws herself back in her chair and there's a silence between them.

Red doesn't look up from the tabletop. "Was there anyone in that room?" he murmurs. Freya feels her heart rate accelerate and she turns cold. "Was there a girl in that room, Freya?"

"The room was empty, I told you." Freya's face freezes as Red gauges it.

"Okay. Well, it's not a suicide mission when you have no choice." He points at Freya's wrist accelerator. "They'll send us anywhere they want, and whenever they want. And we're going to India."

THIRTY-ONE

His bones tingle as if a low current is passing through them. Tomato is not much of a rumor mill—it's way too professional for that. Yet, he's heard things. That they located Te Wiata. Not the kid over the ridge but the old, evil bastard they were out to kill.

Dart enters the conference room. A tall, lean man in a tweed jacket, an archetypical college professor type, is standing with his back to the plate-glass window. His nose is long and thin, and from eyes that are sunk deep into his skull, he's surveying Dart like a zoo exhibit. The door opens and Joad enters, followed by Max. They're finishing up a conversation and at first don't acknowledge Dart or the professor. Then Joad turns to them and smiles. "We've found them," he says. "Sit down." The four sit sparsely around a large, highly polished oval conference table.

"Where?" Dart asks.

"Slow down, Darty," Max says with a grin. "Have you two met?"

"No," the professor says, extending the word as if it's laden with curiosity.

"James Hay meet Dart Bevan," she says, using the name he prefers.

Dart presses the question. "Where are they?"

"Okay," Joad says. "Where our mole acceled to is 750 CE, north of England."

"You're certain?"

"Yes, but there's an anomaly. The destination seems to be several hundred feet below grade."

"Underground? Could that be wrong?" Dart asks.

"No," Max replies for Joad. "It's not wrong."

"They could have just acceled your mole right into a grave."

"Seems unlikely," Joad says. "Te Wiata is building up, not cutting down."

"Exactly," Max says. "What's likely is that Te Wiata's base is underground. Low or no visibility to curious neighbors, and they're bound to have neighbors at that location."

"So when do we leave?" Dart asks.

Joad arches his eyebrows. "Whoa, put the brakes on. *We* are not leaving."

"No, no." Dart shakes his head. "I'm on this mission."

"I can think of plenty of reasons why you're not," Joad says. "For one, we need experienced operatives on it."

"TMA is telling me about experienced operatives? You mostly sit on your asses behind screens. I've been on a hundred missions. It's what Allfours do."

"We know what Allfours do, Darty," Max says.

"And Te Wiata knows you. You're the guy who shot his mouth off."

"I'll grow a beard or something. I won't be recognizable." Joad and Max exchange an amused glance. "I'm going."

Joad walks to the window and looks out at the empty blue sky. "I know what you feel like, Casy. I've sort of been there myself." He turns and looks at his son. "But this is a reconnaissance mission only, not a rescue. We need to figure out the lay of the land. There's more to this than rescuing Kaira."

"So who are you sending?"

"Max and Mr. Hay here." Dart can't conceal his incredulity. "Max is a TMA field operative, Dart. Best I know." Dart looks at her and she gives him a *now you know* smile. She's the very antithesis of what he'd expect an operative to be—the tight, restrained, merciless type who'd do anything that needed to get done, like short-charging Porthos. "And James speaks the language."

"What language?"

"Old English."

"What? I can get by in old English," Dart says. "We don't need that." Hay's smile is faint but enough to convey the intended contempt.

"Come on, I can follow a fucking Shakespeare plot." Now everyone but Dart is grinning.

"Casy," Joad says. "Shakespeare is modern English. We're looking at a destination almost a thousand years earlier. James speaks and understands Anglo-Saxon, and in the right dialect for the where and when."

"Why do we need that? Te Wiata's cronies aren't going to be—"

"Because," Max interrupts, "we can't accel through the tachyon shield that's protecting them, so we'll need to land outside of it. And probably a fair ways outside to reduce the chances they'll detect a bow wave or an arrival. And we've no idea where to access Te Wiata's base. To have a chance in hell we'll need local help. We'll need to speak the language and *what light through yonder window breaks* ain't gonna cut it, Darty." Dart repositions himself in his seat to burn off some anger.

Joad's expression softens. "Let me ask you something, Casy. How sure are you that Kaira isn't there because she wants to be?"

Dart takes a deep breath and blows it out to calm himself. His natural inclination to rage at this point won't help him. "If you think that, why would you bother getting her out?"

"I don't think anything, I'm just asking. And we'd bother getting her out because she has value to Te Wiata."

"Okay. Look ..." Dart continues. "I need to go. Staying here is not an option. One way or another, I'm out of this place. And if the reason I leave is anything but this mission, then we're done." Dart glares into his father's face. "We're done."

THIRTY-TWO

She hears the door lock behind them. Lying on a bench in the middle of the small, dank cave are two weapons: a semi-automatic handgun and a sniper rifle.

"No clothes? We're doing a negative accel of two-and-a-half thousand years dressed like this?" Freya says. "It's almost as if they want us dead."

Recently, Red has had no receptors for irony. "We'll be in and out," he says. Freya begins to protest but checks herself. In the scheme of things, this is a small grievance. Besides, if she's going to be speared through the gut, she'd rather go in comfortable clothing.

"Here's the plan," Red says, inspecting his rifle. "I take out the ancestor. He's been identified for me. You're going to cover me." Freya raises her eyebrows. "Take out anyone who even looks like they may be a threat."

She shakes her head in disbelief. "We're about to be plunged into the middle of an ancient battle. Do you really think there'll be a threat? Where will we land? And how do we get back?"

"You press the accelerator button. That's a *Return Request*."

"A return *request*?" Freya says incredulously. "So I ask

'Would you mind popping me out from the middle of this pitched battle, if it's not too much trouble?' What if the request is denied?" Red hands the pistol to Freya, who now knows how to rack it.

"Okay, back-to-back, weapon raised and ready to fire." Freya follows the instruction. "Ready," Red calls out, but to whom, Freya doesn't know. She holds her breath.

It always takes a second to register surroundings. This can be the most terrifying second in an accel because no matter how fast a thinker, or how prepared with a cocked weapon, the traveler is completely vulnerable. They dive to the ground. It's daytime, and flat on their bellies all they see is the dusty incline in front of them. There's shouting coming from beyond the hilltop, and from farther away the distant trumpeting of elephants. Or, at least, that's Freya's best guess.

Weapon over shoulder, Red army-crawls up the slope and Freya follows. When they reach the crest the scene before them is on a scale she hadn't imagined. A line of chariots, motionless but for the restless horses, begins at the bottom of the incline, extending to the horizon, with blocks of regimented soldiers trailing behind them, standing in silence. The men, in their thousands, are carrying spears and shields. This must be the left flank of the battle formation. She looks along the army's line of sight and sees a cloud of dust obscuring whatever is under it. The cloud is making its way towards the motionless army, and the sounds of battle are getting closer.

"There he is, just like they said," Red says.

"Who?"

"The commander we're after—he's right there on the far-left flank." The closest chariot, maybe a hundred feet away, is bigger than any she'd ever seen. There are four horses harnessed to it and five men positioned inside—four archers and the fifth who's holding the reins, all clad in gold chain mail and domed helmets. The side of the chariot is protected by a sheet of gold armor emblazoned with a yellow sun on a red background.

"The sun. That's him. That's the bastard." Red removes his rifle from his shoulder, folds down the bipod, and rests the gun on the hilltop. He positions the sight and places his finger on the trigger. Freya can make out the red sighting laser on its target. The chariot lurches forward and the commander pulls the reins. "Shit."

"Let's not do this and say we did, Red," Freya says. He looks up from the sight.

"If we go back and Kaira ..." He looks back down the sight, aims, and pulls the trigger. One of the archers falls. "Fuck. We need to get closer."

"Closer? Are you crazy? We could almost pet the horses."

"I move in, take the shot, we hit the accel request, and pop out of here. It's that easy. We're not going to fail this time."

Before Freya can respond, Red begins to crawl down the far side of the incline. If anyone had bothered to look their way, he'd be in full view. But the army's attention is on the approaching cloud, heralded by men screaming and elephants trumpeting. Red takes a second shot but this time he misses.

Before he can try again, the beasts burst out of the cloud, covered in full armor. The soldiers atop them are clutching onto the riding towers as their bodies are shaken like rag dolls while others are being flung to the ground. Men are running ahead of the animals until they're trampled or gored or tossed aside by metal-clad tusks.

If orders were being given, they couldn't possibly have been heard, but some of the chariots begin to move forward, and others follow. Their plan could only have been to navigate between the retreating war elephants and confront the pursuing invaders, but within seconds the vanguard of chariots is being smashed like toys, tossed aside effortlessly.

Freya's pistol is beyond pathetic in the midst of this nightmare of armored giants, horsed chariots, and human carnage. She has the right to be shaking and screaming, but instead she's experiencing an inexplicable calm—a pragmatic sense of survival. Down below Red is still trying to find the golden chariot amidst the tumult, and now she propels herself down the incline, throwing herself to the ground beside him. She's about to shout something over the din when she feels the earth tremble under her.

Looking up, there's an armor-clad monster barreling towards them, and it's bellowing with a cutting loudness she hadn't imagined a living thing could produce. Behind the beast are soldiers on horseback, allowing it to clear their path.

"We're done," Freya yells, although Red would, at best, only see moving lips. She raises her wrist and hopes to god that the *Return Request* isn't just a comfort feature and that someone deigns to respond. Red grabs her other hand and shakes his head. He must want to be trampled to mush rather than face Te Wiata. She pulls hard but he has the grip of a madman. The elephant, so close now that she can smell its rotten breath, is a pace from crushing their bones into the dirt.

With her free hand, she grips Red's accelerator, the ball of her thumb on the return button. Her thoughts are fast but clear. The tachyon blast radius may not encompass her, and she might be about to leave her ass or other extremities behind, or the Return Request might not even work. But this is a decision without real options—they're about to be pancaked. She squeezes and they pop, leaving the beast's foot to crater the ground that had been under them.

THIRTY-THREE

Max has no compunction about immodesty and strips down to don the period clothing. Dart looks at his father who smiles in a *that's Max for you* way. She slides a white gown over her head that unfolds to the floor, and over it places a blue woolen wrap she ties off at the waist. Finally she puts on the white wimple, which covers her hair and neck.

Dart turns his back to the group and remove his jeans and T-shirt. He can feel the grins at his back. He puts on the loose trousers and Hay helps him tie the cross garters. Next, the linen undershirt, and then the long overshirt with a sleeve that's loose enough to accommodate an accelerator. The final touches are a leather belt and soft-bottomed, ill-fitting shoes. Then Hay hands Dart a sack full of something heavy.

"You don't open your mouth, Dart. Not a syllable," Max says. "You're a Dane who can't speak a word of Anglo-Saxon. Got that?"

"What's in the sack?"

"Amber jewelry. We're traders. You get to carry it so you're not completely useless," she replies, tucking a dagger into Dart's belt.

Joad puts a hand on Dart's shoulder and brings his face

close to his son's, which now sports an unkempt beard. "It's a reconnaissance mission. That's all it is, Casy. You try anything even slightly dumb and Max has authority to kick your ass. The mission is to find the access points to Te Wiata's base, and then you come home."

"And then what? You send in some of your more macho tackychemists to assault the base?"

"Casy," Joad replies, "we have the full force of the United States federal government behind us. We send in whoever we need to send in. Okay?"

All that now remains on the table are three handguns.

"In case the dagger doesn't do it," Joad says.

At the far end of the accel it's twilight. They're standing in a field of crops that are swaying in a chilly wind, and Dart smells burning wood.

"There it is," Hay says, pointing to something behind Dart. "The village of Sveinfolk." A hundred yards away, beyond the edge of the crop field, stands a haphazard collection of small buildings. They have uneven wooden planks for walls, thatched straw for roofs, and there's smoke rising from them. "A couple of hundred residents at most."

"Okay, Darty, you know the rules. You just follow. You don't have any ideas. You don't speak. And if you can manage it, you don't think. C'mon." Max sets off towards the village and they follow. As they approach, the smell of burning wood becomes suffused with a nasty aroma. Dart knows exactly what it is. It's cabbage—a smell that has made him gag since childhood.

He's not sure how any of this is going to work. Is Hay going to ask some local where the entrance is to a renegade's evil lair? That'll be sure to work. It occurs to Dart that most of his outings as an Allfour were to kill someone, so a mission that exceeds the subtlety of a shooting is quite new to him.

Max stops and halts the others, waving them to kneel in

the tall crops. A few yards ahead, next to the closest building, there are two men. And there's laughter. At their feet is a woman. As one man climbs onto her, the other kneels to help pin her down. She's struggling, and one of the men yelps as if bitten. Without discussion, Dart stands and sets off towards them.

"Hey, Sir Galahad," Max hisses, grabbing his heel, "get down."

He crouches. He's used to calling the shots.

"I'll deal with this," she says. "You've forgotten the fucking rules already? You're doing what you're told. Because if that doesn't happen, we're turning this car right around and you're going home to Daddy." He looks at her defiantly but backs down. "Now, just plant your heroic ass right here," she says, then stands and sets off towards the men.

"Can she even speak the lingo?" Dart asks Hay. He shakes his head. "Then what the hell is she going to do? Give them a withering look?"

"You don't know Max too well, do you?"

"You mean a woman is going to take out two men in merry old England? They'll have her as a witch and the mission will be over."

"Maybe, if there are survivors. Anyway, point of fact: this is long before witches got a bad rap. In this period, they were healers."

"She's not walking like someone who's about to heal," Dart says.

One of the men notices Max approaching and stands upright, as if judging whether they may have some bonus prey. The other looks like he won't be disturbed and stays on top of his victim. Max looks like she's saying something to them, but she can't be.

Then there's an audible crack as Max delivers a high kick to the man's jaw. He drops vertically to the ground, probably unconscious before he lands. As the second man starts to pull himself up from the woman, Max crouches and does something to him that Dart can't make out, but it's enough to keep him down and out until the woman has time to run away.

"So is that it? Mission screwed?" Dart asks.

"Depends who they were," Hay replies. "Maybe we just saved the Chieftain's daughter."

"Or maybe Max just kicked the shit out of the Chieftain."

THIRTY-FOUR

Red releases his grip on Freya's wrist and they lie in the cave, panting. The sudden silence is deafening, and Freya presses her palms to her ears.

There are two men waiting, one of whom stoops to take their weapons, and without a word, they exit. Red watches them walk away until they vanish around a curve in the corridor. A moment passes and he begins to hyperventilate. Freya can't tell whether it's the relief of escaping a trampling, or of not being frog-marched to Te Wiata.

"Why did you do that?" His eyes are glistening with welling tears.

"Because being scraped from the ground by Alexander the Great is something neither of us have ever wanted."

"You think what's going to happen'll be better?"

Freya places her hand on Red's shoulder. "No one who's sane could have expected this mission to succeed. Trust me." She looks down the empty corridor. Maybe they'd survive this day after all.

Freya is lying alone when the tent flap lifts and a big-bearded, fat-faced man in a plaid shirt pokes his head inside.

"Privacy, asshole," Freya says.

"Barry wants to see you."

She takes a breath. There may have been a delay, but she supposes that the comeuppance was inevitable. "Red isn't here. When he—"

"Barry wants to see *you*."

Freya affects a nonchalant shrug and swings her legs over the side of the cot. She follows the lumberjack through the labyrinth of harshly lit rock corridors and after a few minutes they stop outside one of the metallic doors.

It's a surprise. This isn't the troglodytic office where she'd first encountered Te Wiata. It looks more like a space that a regular, modern human would occupy. There are paintings of mountain-strewn landscapes hanging on brightly painted walls, and a faux window with a projection of a babbling brook. There's a highly polished desk and a plush leather couch, where Te Wiata is sitting, arm resting across its back, holding what looks like a crystal glass of whiskey.

There's another person in the room, sitting with her back to Freya. Sarah Bari turns and smiles as Te Wiata gestures for Freya to sit. The only open seat is on the couch, and Freya positions herself up against the arm rest, as far from Te Wiata as practical. This is dizzyingly unanticipated.

"What's your tipple, Freya?" Te Wiata asks. She isn't too indignant to reply. Te Wiata nods knowingly, as if he had gained great insight into her soul by discovering that she favors vodka. There's a framed photograph on the desk. It looks like a young Prasad and a very young Te Wiata sitting on a park bench, sandwiches in hand, and sporting big posed smiles.

Te Wiata hands Freya her drink. "First of all, I need to apologize," he says. "I know these living conditions are far from ideal, and we'll figure out a way to make them better for everyone, but for now, I think most Allfours would say it's worth it." He looks to Sarah for confirmation and gets it. In this warm, soft light, the misery in Sarah's face has gone. Little wonder Sarah had been so tight-lipped. She's part of the inner sanctum.

"I want to talk to you about something. And it's about Athos, too—Red. You know, he came to me a while ago, telling me about the Musketeers and how he thought they could play a bigger role in the Movement."

The little shit, Freya thinks, although this is only confirmation.

"The Musketeers were impressive," he continues. "A lot of solid, successful missions—and I'm always looking for new talent. So I said yes. But, and for reasons I probably don't have to explain to you, I think I'd overestimated Red's potential." Freya sips her vodka. "You, however ... Well, I think you're a different story."

He waits for a response that Freya doesn't provide.

"Sarah has been telling me a lot about you, and I think your role in the Movement could be bigger ... much bigger." Sarah is smiling at Freya. "You're smart, rational, cool under pressure, committed. I don't want to see that wasted, Freya."

She stares into her drink and braces to suppress her first reaction. "Well, yes. I'm complimented."

"Good," he says and chuckles. "So I can't leave you partnered with Red. You'll learn nothing from him. At least nothing good. I want you to partner with Sarah." She looks up at Sarah who's giving her the look of *well how about that?* as if it's a surprise to her, too.

"Yes, great. I'd like that." That had to be the right answer. When you're at rock bottom, change is good.

"Excellent. So you won't be seeing much of Red anymore. I'm moving him out of the dorm. We'll find him a role more befitting his talents. As far as you're concerned, he's gone. That okay?"

Freya doesn't know what *gone* means, and as repulsive as Red has become to her, there are limits on what she'd wish on him. "That's fine, Dr. Te Wiata."

"Stop it. *Barry*, please. Oh, and before you leave, there's one more thing."

The door swishes open and Kaira enters, her diaphanous, powder blue sari floating as she walks. Freya needs to look like she's taking all of this in her stride, but she's betrayed by a broad smile.

"I know you've been missing your fellow Musketeer."

Freya stands. She and Kaira look at each other and, hesitantly, shake hands. Te Wiata laughs. Kaira shows no signs of abuse or of even tough living; in fact, she looks radiant.

"I'm sorry to have hidden her away, but she needs to be safe." *Safe* seems like a strange word to Freya, given Kaira's role as disposable litmus paper. "But you'll have full access to each other from now on."

THIRTY-FIVE

"And now what?" Dart asks.

"Now we go straight to the top," Hay says. "You have quality goods in that bag, and it'd be an insult to give first viewing to anyone but the Chieftain."

They navigate the small cottages of wood and thatched straw. There's no logic to the layout of the village—nothing that could be considered a street or a gathering area. A young, giggling couple run by them, giving more attention to each other than to the strangers. Then what looks to Dart like an old man (although he'd learned that aging someone from a different era can be perilous) appears at the door of a cottage. He's eyeing the travelers as smoke from the building escapes around him. Hay walks toward the old man, who takes a step back, and they begin to speak. It's incomprehensible to Dart but it has the old man's attention.

"So that's the language you're fluent in, is it?" Max says.

"That's English? That's not English." The temperature is dropping and Dart would be happy to step into a smokey house reeking of cabbage just to warm up. The incomprehensible conversation continues until the old man points at something and then watches Hay suspiciously as he walks away.

They follow Hay. This house is bigger than the others, with a row of skulls hanging over the entrance and two bulky men skulking outside. They notice the travelers and walk towards them with the timeless swagger of menace. Hay grabs the bag from Dart and tells him to stay back. One of the men is transfixed on Max. This could be a bad day for him depending on what thoughts are behind that look, and in a pinch, Dart thinks he could take the other guy. They start talking and Hay opens the bag. One of the men peers inside.

"Give them your daggers," Hay says, beckoning Max and Dart over.

They're led to the house. Inside, the smell of cooking cabbage is so overwhelming, Dart could chew it. He swallows rapidly to suppress the gag reaction. He knows nothing of early medieval culture but projectile vomiting as you enter the Chieftain's home is probably more bad than good. The cottage is illuminated by a long fire pit bordered by stones, and pots are cooking on it. As his eyes acclimatize, he sees maybe a dozen people crammed into the space, from small children to decrepitly old adults. The floor is covered with straw and there are a few items of simple wooden furniture—a table, chairs, a trunk. If this is how a chieftain lives, Dart can only imagine the lifestyle of regular peasants. An old man occupies one of the chairs, flanked by a younger man and woman. Behind the old guy is a woman who could be his wife and she's holding the hand of a young boy.

Hay bows to the seated man, so Dart and Max do the same. Dart looks over his shoulder and sees the two bruisers looking on. The rest of the house's occupants have stepped back to give the strangers room. Hay begins to speak. He says something that causes everyone to look in Dart's direction. Then the old man says something to Hay.

"You're in luck," Hay says quietly to Dart. "There's another Dane visiting the village."

Shit! Dart smiles at the old man.

"This is Chieftain Svein." Dart and Max bow again and the young girl giggles. Is bowing the wrong thing? Or can you just do too much of it? A few more words are exchanged. This guy Hay is good. Allfours never had the motivation to acquire such skills, but then if your main objective is to shoot someone, a chat isn't always necessary.

Hay tips the bag onto the surface of the table. There are polished amber beads, necklaces and bracelets of threaded amber chips, amber pendants and brooches, amber strap ends and other unrecognizable items of jewelry. There's a collective gasp and Dart takes this to mean they're impressed by this collection of crap. As the Chieftain's family paws the goods, Dart notices that he's being watched closely by the girl who had been at the Chieftain's side. She sees that she has his attention and smiles. Dart flashes an embarrassed smile back.

"I think you're in there, Darty," Max whispers. "You better be home before midnight, and remember to take precautions."

"Fuck off," Dart says and Max chuckles.

"So you *do* have some Anglo-Saxon."

Someone else in this reeking, smokey room seems focused on him. The man standing in the shadows is showing no interest in the jewelry, but is definitely fascinated by Dart and Max. He's tall compared to the others, thin-faced, and bald on top with long, yellow stalks of straw for hair. He reminds Dart of the scarecrow on his twentieth-century farm.

Hay is speaking rapidly now. A sales pitch or maybe a negotiation. The professor nods, then walks back to his Danes, leaving the family to try on his wares. He whispers, "I'm consulting you on price. There's someone over there who hasn't taken his eyes off you."

"We noticed," Max says. "I'll watch him."

Hay looks over his shoulder. "We could flog our entire stock tonight."

"Fabulous news, but what now?" Dart asks. "What's

next?"

"Patience," Max says. "Just keep flirting for now."

Hay's snoring is unrelenting. They had been offered a building for the night with the dimensions of a tool shed so that negotiations on the jewelry sales could continue in the morning. The bag of straw is comfortable enough, but Dart is too cold and too full of cabbage to sleep.

"How are you enjoying your first Tomato mission?" Max whispers, as if there were a remote chance of disturbing Hay. Obviously, she can't sleep either.

"Is it going well? I can't tell. Allfour missions are simple, in and out."

"Oh, I know. And someone's left dead." Max sits up, her face crossed by moonlight leaking through gaps in the wall. "So far so good. There'll be a chance to ask the right questions once we have the rapport."

"And how long will that take?"

She doesn't answer. Max glows in the moonlight like some angelic visitor.

"You know, you don't fit my image of a TMA operative," Dart says.

"No?"

"No. You're troublingly affable in a sort of painful way. And you're funny, or at least want to be."

"And TMA operatives can't be like that?"

"No, they're more in the business of short-charging people. Don't get me wrong, you seem violent enough for the job, but it's the other qualities." The snoring stops briefly as Hay adjusts position.

"I know the guy who did that to your friend," Max says. "He was always an asshole. And by the way, he's no longer with TMA. Dealt with." Max lies back and puts her hands behind her head. A cloud covers the moon and they're in complete blackness. "Besides, a recovering Allfour is no one to lecture anyone on violence."

"And you and Te Wiata are really an item? Really?"

"Oh, we're going to do that now?"

"The bastard we're all trying to take out? One of the reasons we're here?"

"We're not here to take anyone out. And yes, we're ... what'd you call it? An item. The Te Wiata on the island is innocent."

Dart shakes his head incredulously, although in the dark, it's only for him. "But knowing what he becomes? Is it that you think you can change him?"

"Well, it seems I haven't done that so far since the timeline hasn't snapped. And no, changing him is not it."

"You could just kill the fucker."

"That's how the Movement works, not TMA." There's a prolonged silence and Dart can't tell if Max is done with this conversation. Then she says, "This is a new world. One where it seems even the laws of logic have shifted. If you're not scared shitless by it then you don't understand it. Even if you are scared shitless, you don't understand it because no one does. And part of this new world is knowing more than we really need to know. Yeah, I know what Barry's going to become. But these are new rules—rules we have to make up as we go along. My Barry Te Wiata is a brilliant guy who's trying to understand a new scientific order on behalf of everyone. The Te Wiata I know is kind, funny—"

"Spare me, Max."

"You're thinking by the old rules, Dart."

"And do you think the older, evil Te Wiata is right about the young one you seem to like? About the Big One? That if he can edit out Prasad the timeline will shift to one where *he's* the hero of tackychemistry?"

"No, I don't. Something happened to Barry. I get that the old Te Wiata is crazy. But what may be true is that without him, Prasad couldn't have done what he did. I've seen them work together, and it's possible. You know, you were born into TMA royalty. It was all handed to you on a big silver platter. But Barry—he taught himself. It was his genius and commitment that got him discovered and plucked by Prasad from some place you've never heard of. He bootstrapped himself to the top."

The moon reappears and Dart shivers. "And you have no problem with the mission of taking him out?"

"I have no problem with that." Her blue eyes are as pale as angelite. "If we don't, then sooner or later he'll do something that changes everything—something that could blink a billion innocent people out of the picture. I know we can't let that happen. I get it." Max turns over. The conversation is over.

THIRTY-SIX

The woman leading Freya through the labyrinth is wearing stilettos. *Who the hell wears stilettos in a cave?* In her tight skirt and low-cut blouse she's dressed like the sexy secretary in a bad sitcom, and she has not once turned to make sure Freya is in tow. Two hours had passed since Te Wiata's invitation to visit Kaira whenever she wanted, and now was that time. They come to a stop at one of the metal doors lining the corridor. The sexy secretary nods at it and continues on her way, not having once acknowledged Freya.

What kind of conversation will this be? Is Kaira really here against her will? How can she be sure?

Yet if Kaira knew her function as a sophisticated litmus test, then there'd be no question about her wanting to stay, would there? But does she know? What would stop Freya from telling her? Little of this new world of a kinder Te Wiata makes any sense. Maybe he figures that because both she and Kaira are captive it really doesn't matter what they know or don't know. And Kaira doesn't know whether Freya is here against her will. So they'll both be working under the assumption that anything said will get back to Te Wiata. Besides, they've probably bugged the hell out of whatever room is behind this door.

Freya places her hand on the door and it opens. Kaira is standing on the other side wearing a wine-red sari tunic. She steps forward and embraces Freya. Freya has never been a hugger yet she'd be okay with this one lasting. Then Kaira takes her hand and leads her to a red velvet couch. The room is bright and warm. There's a bed in the corner, closets along one wall, and paintings of abstract patterns hanging alternately with speakers. This room, which looks like it has been snatched from twenty-first century suburbia, gives no hint of its real location.

"God, I'm glad to see you," Kaira says and then leans in close to Freya, putting her lips against her ear. "Is Dart here?"

Freya's ear tickles. She puts her lips to Kaira's ear and smells her perfume, which is exotic and warm. These past weeks, the only fragrant object Freya had known was the soap in the communal showers, and that smelled like wood shavings. "If he is, I haven't found him yet. He could be sequestered somewhere."

It was Kaira's turn again to put her lips against Freya's ear, and this time she cupped Freya's cheek to keep her close. Freya's heart is pounding. Of course it is—this is risky.

"What about Athos?"

"He's here, but they have him locked up somewhere."

"Why?"

There was no value in truth here. "I don't know." Freya sits back on the couch and speaks for the bugs. "This beats the dorm."

"Does it? I haven't seen the dorm." Kaira pours wine for them. With little shared history, small talk doesn't come easy. Finally, Kaira puts down her wine glass and moves close to Freya, palm to cheek, lips to ear. "I don't know if I can trust you, Freya, but I want you to know something, because I don't think I could make things any worse." Her hand is cool and her breath warm. "I don't want to be here." She lets go of Freya and sits back to gauge her reaction. She leans in again. "Don't get me wrong, I believe in the Movement. I believe in its causes." This surely can't mean to murder Kaira's grandfather and use her to test their success. "But I want to go back to the cottage. To be the kind of Allfour I used to be."

Freya holds Kaira's cheek. "I want out, too. God, do I." She has upped the stakes. "Te Wiata has me on missions ... I'm expendable. I'm nothing." Kaira sits back and surveys Freya. Was this a step too far?

Then Kaira nods and Freya exhales.

"How?" Kaira whispers. "How do we get the fuck out? I mean, who's going to help us do that? The Musketeers are done for. And I doubt that TMA'll bother saving a couple of Allfours who brought all this on themselves."

Freya knows exactly what she shouldn't say, but she says it anyway, their faces nearly touching. "There's hope. I've got reasons." Kaira doesn't reply. She doesn't ask for clarification or explanation. She just smiles as if Freya is only trying to comfort her. The smile was worth the risk.

"Please keep looking for Dart," Kaira whispers. "I can just feel that he's close." Then a tear wets Freya's cheek. "He's close."

THIRTY-SEVEN

Dart wakes with a start and it takes a second to register what he's seeing. Someone is thrashing and gurgling. And it seems to be because Max is kneeling on them. Hay leaps to his feet and barks out some Anglo-Saxon. It's the scarecrow from the Chieftain's house. Words fly quickly back and forth until Hay goes silent, and his eyes widen.

"I'm Allfours," the scarecrow chokes out. Hay pulls up the man's sleeve and there it is: an accelerator. Max grabs his wrist and Hay struggles to remove the device but it won't budge.

"Start saying things that might stop me crushing your windpipe," Max says.

"Surface duty," he says. "I'm on surface duty."

Max's knee presses down on the man's throat. "More."

He coughs and tries to catch his breath. "Just on the lookout."

Max lifts her knee an inch. "And now you report back?"

"Supposed to, yes."

Hay steps back. "How did you know?"

"Don't worry," the scarecrow replies. "Your Anglo-Saxon's perfect. Well, you did use the form 'cnotta' which isn't in use until the ninth century. You should use the

Proto-Germanic 'knuttô', but—" Max lowers her knee and Dart savors the expression on Hay's face. "Okay, I read lips. The three of you weren't conferring in Norse back there."

Max pulls him up and rolls his sleeve down over the accelerator. "And what were you doing in Svein's house?"

"Been doing this a long time and now I'm in Svein's witan. Sort of advisor. Bring a forward-looking view." He manages a weak grin.

"And you dropped by to deal with us?" Max asks.

He hesitates.

"Don't make me regret that you're alive after all these seconds."

"I want out," he blurts.

Max smirks. "*Do* you?"

"Yes. I want out of it. I didn't sign up for this."

"And what *did* you sign up for?" Max asks.

"I've got no love for the TMA dictatorship, but Te Wiata's version of the Movement isn't the one I joined."

"And how do you know we're not Te Wiata's people and that you didn't just cook your own scrawny goose?"

"What would Te Wiata's people be doing selling jewelry on the surface?"

Max grins. "So you want the TMA dictatorship to get you out?"

Dart's patience is thinning and he says, "Is there a physical way in?"

"Let's just—" Hay begins.

"Is there a physical way in?"

"I think so."

"You think so."

"We accel in and out. There's no need for a physical entrance, but I think I've mapped one. Thought it might come in useful one day."

"It's that day," Dart says, not looking up to gauge his colleagues. He knows what he'd see.

"I've traced a route from the inside and one from the outside."

"And?"

"And I'm pretty sure they connect up."

"Pretty sure?" Hay says. "What does that mean? Either—"

"Show us," Dart says.

Max places a hand on Dart's arm which has a *slow-down* feel to it. "How many people under there?" she asks.

"Don't know exactly. Three hundred? Maybe more."

"And how many of them aren't happy about it?"

"Most, I'd say. But there aren't many who'd cross Te Wiata. Mouthy sorts tend to vanish."

"Is there anyone down there from the Musketeers band?" Dart asks. The Allfour shakes his head hesitantly. "Never heard—"

"Can you get us in there?" Dart says.

"Whoa!" Hay interjects. "We're not getting in anywhere. We are in reconnaissance."

"Get us in and we'll help you."

"Not a chance." Hay looks at Max for support.

"That's our mission," Dart says to Hay. "We're here to find a physical entrance to Te Wiata's base. Did you expect to find an archway illuminated with fairy lights and a sign saying *Barry's Secret Grotto*? We don't know it's an entrance until we use it to enter."

Hay shakes his head vigorously. "Max, we don't have time for this. We go back and we report."

Max does not respond quickly enough for Hay who affects incredulity. "The kid's right," she says. "We need to take this one step further."

THIRTY-EIGHT

There had been a marked change in the missions that Freya was being assigned. To say that they were completely unsuicidal would be an exaggeration, but they did offer a solid prospect of returning intact. The sitcom secretary would show up at their tents and give Freya and Sarah mission instructions.

The most violent of their recent tasks had been to pluck a hair from the head of a very old man. This had probably been to feed Te Wiata's Allfours Analytics Team with DNA data for mapping ancestries. It would, no doubt, lead to a murder, but at least that wasn't Freya's job. The provider of the follicle had been in a wheelchair, located in some English-speaking but otherwise indeterminate country, likely around the mid-nineteenth century. As Freya had plucked the hair, the old man cried out, sending her sprawling into an ornate tea table and crashing to the floor. The tea ware and petit fours had followed trajectories that spread them wide across the carpet. Sarah was laughing convulsively when they popped out.

Another mission had been to attend an early lecture given by Marina Logan, one of the two scientists who, in the 1980s, had first observed temporal acceleration. That was a time when there was still talk of it in public, before it had been concertedly ridiculed and the research taken behind secure government doors. Their mission had been to record the lecture. No doubt, it would somehow support Te Wiata's narrative of having a major role in creating the science of tackychemistry. Again, no one had needed to be killed.

One mission had actually excited Freya. It was to be her first acceleration into the future—positive seconds per second, landing her at the end of the twenty-first century. And it had something to do with one of the great open questions of temporal science: the mystery of the tachyon horizon. Excitement for the mission had, for a while, reminded Freya of her old self, exhilarated by the possibility of discovery instead of terrified by the near certainty of death. Why was there a brick wall for tachyons at the end of the twenty-first century—no temporal acceleration across the wall in either direction? That was the mystery. A tachyon interference field had been activated at that time, but the conundrum was who did it and how?

Te Wiata's team had detected an anomaly in the field—a blip in its density that might have had something to do with the field's source—and they had been able to pinpoint that blip. So Freya and Sarah had been sent up-time of the blip to see what they could see. Maybe there would be a shiny facility housing the creators of the field and their fabulous technologies. But there had been a danger. If the field had been activated during their reconnaissance, there'd be no going home. They'd be stranded on the wrong side of the brick wall.

With the accel, Freya and Sarah found themselves in blistering heat, surrounded by cacti and bush. Te Wiata hadn't had the courtesy to tell them where they were going, but this looked like the deserts of New Mexico that Freya had once visited. There was a mountain range in the distance and a hot wind that blew dust into her eyes while doing little to cool her.

Freya had a pretty good idea why Te Wiata was so interested in the tachyon horizon. If he were to get his hands on the technological bounties beyond it, then the world would be his oyster. She doubted he had any abstract interest in the science and the mystery. On the other hand, Freya *did* have an interest. Why is the global shield located at the end of the twenty-first century in particular? Who could have had pulled it off? Or maybe they acceled back from some far-flung future to create the shield. But then why do it at the end of the twenty-first? Why not install the barrier a century earlier to cut off temporal acceleration at the pass? That would have prevented any travel backward in time right from the inception of the technology. What a logical quagmire that would have prevented.

But the mission had been a bust. Nothing to see. No shining facility. It had amused Freya to think that Red would have been crapping himself at the failure, but this now seemed to be a new world in which they could afford to disappoint Te Wiata. At least for now.

THIRTY-NINE

First light is turning the sky to steel gray. They have been walking for an hour and Dart is shivering, breathing vapor into the frigid air. Max looks back to make sure the group is in tow while the Allfour walks ahead, leading them through a heavily wooded area that would be an ideal place for an ambush. But why bother with all of this just for an ambush? There must have been easier ways to capture or kill them.

Dart is counting his top one hundred uncertainties. The first on the list had been triggered by something Joad had asked. How sure was he that Kaira is being held against her will? He hadn't dared give his father an honest answer. Kaira had never shown any doubt about the Allfours' cause. Maybe she hadn't been as strident as Athos, and she often stood up to defend Dart, but that was more about protecting him than any chinks in her commitment. What if they're trying to rescue someone who doesn't need rescuing? No, he wouldn't go there. If he wants to anguish about uncertainties, he's spoiled for choice and won't pick that one.

If he finds and rescues Kaira, then what? What is his life? What is *their* life after that? He's gone from a promising young TMA physicist, to Allfours rebel, to Allfours cynic, to third-rate TMA operative. Which Dart, or Casy, comes out the back end of this? What other U-turns, twists, and transformations lie ahead for someone who can't make a good decision to save his life, but who sure as hell knows how to make a drastic one? Wherever he goes, it'll have nothing to do with tackychemistry and any time travel bullshit. But what the hell does he know about anything outside of that world? He'd be hard-pressed to even list the types of jobs that people do, let alone actually do any of them. Baker? Roofer? Falconer?

Dart smiles. He's never considered himself an optimist but thinking about what follows this mission and his possible life as a roofer is the very essence of optimism.

"Earth to Dart," he hears. "You with us?" Max is grinning at him. "You were deep in thought there, Darty. Why don't you stick to something you're actually good at?" She points at the Allfour who's standing next to what looks like an earth mound. "It's an air shaft," she says. "Getting close. My accelerator's dead as a doornail, so we must be inside the interference shield."

"The air shaft's an access point," Dart says. "We can get down there."

"I doubt that," Scarecrow says. "It must be a known vulnerability and I'm guessing it's heavily protected. Probably sensors connected to tachyon guns that'll open up the shield just long enough to fling our torsos to the Jurassic. I'd avoid that option."

"So where is the access point?"

The Allfour points further up the slope.

"You don't need reminding," Max says, "but if you're fucking with us, having your dick acceled to the Jurassic will have seemed the better option." Scarecrow waits to see if Max has finished her threat, then turns and continues the ascent. After a few minutes, he stops and the others catch up. Then they see it. At the bottom of the far slope is what's unmistakably a cave entrance. It's an arched opening cut into the mossy limestone, maybe four feet across and half again as high.

"Okay, this is it. Mission accomplished," Hay says.

"This is what?" Dart replies. "It's a hole in a rock wall. Our mission is to find a way into Te Wiata's base."

"We saw the air shaft. We're over the base. We've seen a possible physical entrance. We're done." Hay is appealing to Max and not taking on the futile task of addressing Dart.

Max looks at the Allfour. "How sure are you this connects with the inner side of your route?"

"Eighty-five percent."

Max smirks. "Well, there's a number. Hay, you're going to go back and report out." He starts to protest and she adds, "We won't be needing Anglo-Saxon from here."

"The mission is—"

"Is what I say it is now we're in the field." It seems Max has rank she can pull. "All we've found is a way into something. We need confirmation. That's your explanation, Hay, and your order is, *piss off.*"

He looks at Dart, back at Max, and shrugs. "Yes ma'am." He turns and starts to walk back, shaking his head as he mutters something to himself.

"He's probably right," Max says. "I'm going out on a limb here, but if we don't confirm that this gets us into the base, then that mission goes to someone else." The Allfour is listening attentively. "And if this asshole is screwing with us," she says at him, "I don't want to give anyone else the pleasure of dealing with it."

The slope is steep and Dart, Max, and the Allfour slide down it on their rears. The closer they get, the smaller the opening seems. At first, the inside looks pitch black, but closer in, Dart makes out the pale interior rock, dimly illuminated by the gray morning light. He's the first to step inside. The cave opens up to a space about the size of a two-car garage. He looks back to see Max pushing the Allfour ahead of her.

It feels like his head has been jogged violently without taking his brain with it. There's a flash of bright blue and he falls against the cave wall, searing pain radiating down to his shoulders. The man holding the rock approaches him to deliver a second blow, eyes wild and matted hair pointing in every direction. Dart launches himself forward and grabs the attacker's arm, which neither of them had seemed to expect. Dart balls his fist and slams it into the wild man's abdomen. The man doubles over and falls to his knees.

Max grabs Scarecrow by the shirt, who pushes her away indignantly. With blurring speed, she punches the Allfour in the face and his head snaps back as he collapses. She advances a step, towering over him, and the Allfour holds up a hand, feebly.

"I don't know who this is," he shouts before another blow lands. Max has racked her pistol and is alternating the barrel between the two men. The wild-haired man begins to speak rapidly, the pitch of his voice undulating as if to emphasize his point, whatever it is. The Allfour, momentarily distracted from nursing his bloodied nose, barks a chortle. "He says this is *his* home and that we need to fuck off."

Dart lifts the man's sleeve. No accelerator. He touches his own cheek gingerly.

"You okay?" Max asks.

"Apart from the pain, and maybe a couple of loose teeth."

"No blood at least."

She turns to the Allfour. "A shame. I thought this was my chance to clap you."

The Allfour stumbles to his feet. "You going to deal with him?" he asks.

"Deal with him?" Dart says. "You mean kill him?"

"Why take a risk?"

"What risk? What do you think he's going to do?" Dart looks at the scarecrow and the contempt he feels is as much for himself as for the Allfour, because he was once one of them. That used to be him.

"He just tried to crack your skull open."

Dart looks around. The only candidate for the beginning of a passageway deeper into the cave is what looks like an oversized mousehole in the pale rock.

"That your way in?" he asks the Allfour. "It's pitch black."

Scarecrow looks at Max as if for permission. He ducks into the darkness of the opening. Bright light suddenly spills out and Scarecrow re-emerges holding a big silver flashlight.

"Won't get far without this."

The hermit is staring at them in wide-eyed terror. In that darkness lie spirits and demons, no doubt. He takes a few steps backwards, making some kind of sign with a fist and an open palm, then dashes out into the daylight.

"He has a point," Max says, leaning on the cave wall. "So let's get on with this." Taking the dagger from her belt, she hikes up her gown and begins to cut at it. "Who'd have guessed that the son of Joad Bevan is a little voyeur pervert," she says, grinning at him.

He wishes he'd thought to turn away sooner.

"Nah. Perverts get pleasure out of it."

"Yeah. Tell your pants that."

FORTY

Freya looks up to see Te Wiata's oafs surveying the dorm camp from their balconies. Some seem dazed, staring out in a fixed direction, while others are sharing jokes and trying to outlaugh each other. With a candidate pool for security staff comprised of Allfours, these imbeciles must be the best that can be mustered.

Freya opens the flap and ducks into the tent. Sarah is sitting on her cot, grinning stupidly. "Got it?" Sarah asks.

Freya takes the bottle of vodka out of her pocket and wags it in Sarah's face. "Praise be to Kaira. Apart from the splash I had with you and Te Wiata, I haven't had a snort in a year."

"Yeah. I could almost forgive Te Wiata for some things, but withholding this? Asshole." Sarah reaches down and removes a bucket from beneath her cot. It's full of ice.

"Nice!" Freya pours, they clink cups, they gulp, and they cough. "Oh, that's welcome." Freya gets onto the cot and they sit at opposite ends, legs entwined.

"Like the old days," Sarah says.

"Is it? Did we do this in the old days?"

"No, you're right, we didn't. And the days aren't that old to you, are they?"

After refills, talk of Risley turns to recent events. Why had even the boondoggle missions become less frequent? Freya had taken to wandering around the caverns with a nominal goal of finding Dart, but she knew that wouldn't happen.

Another refill and Freya considers herself to be in the zone. That sweet spot beyond inhibition but before collapse. As she gets happier, the vodka seems to be having the opposite effect on Sarah. She had known people like that, but you're seldom aware that you're with one of them until it's too late. Still, Freya decides to stay around for one last refill.

"M'tired," Sarah murmurs.

"Tired? What have you been doing but sitting on your ass?"

"I don't mean that. I mean *tired*. I feel old and I don't know what I'm doing ... don't know ... don't know." Every muscle in her face sags and the bags under her eyes take on a dark, shiny quality.

"But it's for the cause, right?"

Sarah looks up at Freya. "Yeah, the cause. Plucking a hair from that old bastard was for the cause, but when you don't know why it helps the cause, it's hard to have passion, isn't it?"

Freya nods, smiling at the memory.

"I've been in this fucking cave for a year, Freya. And I think I may be going crazy. Am I? I am."

Freya tops up Sarah's cup. "There must be a lot of Allfours who've had enough of this. No matter how much you believe in the cause, you can't live this way. Especially not Allfours who've dumped TMA and joined up because they're all about freedom. They must want out."

"Not everyone's happy, you're right about that." Sarah looks down at her wrist. "You don't get these things locked on you because you're thrilled to be here. And I'm guessing

Te Wiata can be a nasty bastard. Cross him and you put everything at risk: you, your family, family you didn't even know you had, family who are the reason you exist. I've no evidence for any of that, but who's going to take the risk? Look at how he's trying to deal with Prasad."

"So everyone stays put? Doesn't even try to get out?" Freya asks.

"Yeah, and they have the promise of better days ahead, after the Big One. Whatever the fuck that is. It's easy to have faith in something when you've got no choice."

"Do you have faith in the Big One?"

Sarah grins savagely. "You're funny. Look, I'm going to tell you something. I'm at rock bottom, and if Te Wiata could make things any worse for me, then good luck to the fucker. Maybe he could short-charge me and send my bowels to Byzantium, or just vanish me from the timeline, but I'm not sure those things would be any worse. Maybe even better."

Freya smiles. She can still make out the young Sarah in there. The dryad she'd known at TMA, now hiding behind a fog of decades and booze. She can still see her. That Sarah could find positivity in a car wreck.

"I have a way out—for both of us if you're in," Sarah says. "Been a plan for a long time but never had the balls to try it. But now ... now I have no more shits left to give."

Freya knows she should be very careful at this point, but she also knows that her heart wouldn't be in it. "Talk."

"Okay." Sarah pauses. Is it hesitancy or just the struggle to form sentences? "Say we had an accelerator. A real one— not one of these fucking slave units." She shakes her accelerator in Freya's face. "A real one we can program."

Freya's thoughts go to the Dickens character who had confiscated her accelerator and locked this piece of shit onto her. Freya shivers.

"So the plan is, when we're out on our next bullshit mission, outside the shield, we'd use it—the real one."

"You have an accelerator? That seems critical to the

plan."

"Maybe I do." Sarah nods the *do*.

"Okay. So what stops them acceling us right back here with our slave units?"

"Well ... it's not a perfect plan. When we land we'll need to get these slave units off us pronto, or get ourselves behind a shield, at least before anyone figures out we aren't where we're supposed to be. Te Wiata's operations aren't *that* efficient. We'll have a window."

"Behind a shield? That'd mean TMA."

"Yeah, I know. Maybe throwing ourselves on their mercy? What are they going to do to us?"

"And Kaira?" Freya says.

Sarah hesitates too long for Freya. "You're drinking her vodka." They each take another swig. "Do you trust her?" Freya nods and Sarah blinks her glassy eyes. "Okay. Princess Kaira goes with us."

"How do we get her outside the shield?"

Balancing her cup on her chest, Sarah hiccups and ponders the question. "She wasn't part of the plan."

"And even if we could get her outside the shield, one tachyon blast to transport three of us is pushing our luck, isn't it? Something's sure to get left behind. Something grisly." Freya tries to suppress a hiccup but can't. "But if you got your hands on an accelerator, you can get more, right?"

"No." Sarah shakes her head slowly. She rolls onto her stomach and reaches under the cot. There's some fumbling and then she struggles back up, holding a black box. She places it on the cot and swings open the lid.

"Shit," Freya says. "Where'd you get it?"

Sarah grins. "It's the one I arrived with."

Freya runs her finger along the length of the control unit and up the small pods containing the magical chemicals. "Will it still work?" Freya's heart is thudding. "How did you get to keep it? Sarah? How did you get to ...?"

Freya looks up as Sarah begins to snore.

FORTY-ONE

They're crouched in a tunnel barely wide enough for them. The Allfour illuminates the way with his flashlight, followed by Dart, then Max. The air is cold and wet, and a narrow stream of water trickling between their feet seems to be on the same journey.

"This is comfortable," Dart says.

"Stop whining, Darty. At least you don't have to look at your ass."

And what if Kaira doesn't want to be rescued? Dart invites this thought to return just to take his mind off the claustrophobia and his aching back, but it's a bad idea. What would he do? Snatch her anyway? That isn't who he is. Maybe they could turn it into a mission to find Te Wiata and put a bullet in him. But that's not who he is either, not that he'd have a chance in hell of getting the opportunity.

"It's about to get narrower," Scarecrow says.

How is that even possible?

"But at least you'll be able to stand up straight. When we get there, you put your back to the right-side wall and shuffle along sideways. Okay?"

The Allfour had been right. They can now stand as the walls flatten and sandwich them. There can't be three inches between the tip of Dart's nose and the shear rock wall in front of him, from which he can feel his breath reflected. It seems that even when you've only ever experienced mild claustrophobia, a situation extreme enough can bring on a full panic attack.

There are horrific scenarios. If Scarecrow decides to take off ahead, Dart will be pretty much buried alive in the dark. Or if Scarecrow's flashlight fails, or if the battery just runs out ... Dart begins to hyperventilate, the exhaled breath blasting back into his face. He hears grunts that can only be coming from his own mouth. *Keep it together. Keep it together.*

"You okay there, Darty?"

"Yeah. Yeah, I'm okay." Max's voice is a comfort. "How much longer is it this narrow?"

"A few minutes," the Allfour replies in a matter-of-fact voice, seemingly oblivious to these horrendous conditions. They continue to slide forward and Dart is able to get his breathing under control. He discovers that it helps to look upward—a direction in which they're not noticeably trapped—although contact between his chin and the rock wall limits the angle he can achieve.

"Okay," Scarecrow says, "the good news is that the passage is going to get a lot wider. The bad news is that the path isn't. Keep your back to the wall and don't look down, not that you'd see much. The ledge is about a foot wide, so I'll keep my flashlight on it."

"How far is the drop?" Dart asks.

"Makes no difference after fifty feet, does it? And it's a lot more than that."

"How the fuck did you discover this route?" Max asks.

"Desperation."

The journey is a test of every phobia, although death by fall is lower on Dart's list of horrors than live burial. They edge along the path, and the small rocks they displace take a long time to sound their landings. The ledge eventually widens and when Scarecrow shines his flashlight ahead, something momentarily reflects the light right back at them. It's metallic. One after another, they step onto wide, solid ground and Dart's body is flooded with relief. He'd be happy to stand right there forever and die of something appealing like starvation or old age. The circle of illumination from Scarecrow's flashlight passes over several metal objects before Dart snatches it from him.

"What's all this?" Max asks.

"Language is my thing," the Allfour replies. "No clue."

"Dart?"

There's a large metal cube about eight feet tall with three small metal cabinets next to it. Dart stares at them. What *is* all of this? The flashlight produces a tight beam and it's tough to get a sense of the full layout—how it pieces together. He scans a wider arc. Against the far wall of the cavern there are three cylinders, each at least twenty feet high and six feet in diameter, and overhead pipes lead from them into the central metal cube.

"This is tackychemistry," Dart says. "It's an accelerator. Industrial scale: you could accel an aircraft carrier with this."

"Well, we're in the right place, then," Max says.

Dart raises the light to the top of the central cube and sees an array of about twenty narrow bars projecting maybe six feet upward.

"No, wait. I take it back. That's a multi-quadrupole topological phase analyzer." He hears the sounds of impatience. "It's not an accelerator. It's their tachyon interference shield. This'll be connected to a tachyon detection array someplace. Detect an unsanctioned tachyon stream and this thing pipes up. Those bars create a tachyon field in exact anti-phase, canceling out a transportation stream. No one gets in or out."

Dart's mind races. *So what are the implications of standing right next to this?* "Those cabinets are the electrical switchgear and relays." He shines the flashlight on them. "Although it looks like it's controlled remotely." He pulls on a cabinet door and it opens freely. Inside are wires, transistor boards, and other microelectronic circuitry.

"If a rock happens to come into contact with that stuff, I'm guessing the shield goes down," Max says.

"They've got to be monitoring that," Scarecrow says. "Do something to the base's protections and alarms are going to be set off."

"He's right," Dart says. "But I tell you this: acceling out of here with Kaira is an option that's a hell of a lot more attractive than coming back the same way."

With a processing delay, Scarecrow glances at Dart. "That's what all this is for? Rescuing Prasad's granddaughter?"

Dart shines the flashlight in the Allfour's face. "How much further?"

"This is as far as I've gotten from the outside. But ..." They follow him as he takes them to a smoothly crafted opening in the cave wall. "This is an elevator shaft," he says, pointing to a metal panel next to the opening.

"Shit," Dart says.

"So we just need to call for an elevator?" Max asks.

"Wouldn't advise that. It'll be monitored. But look." Dart follows the direction of Scarecrow's finger with his flashlight. "A ladder."

Dart traces it down with the flashlight beam and, squinting, convinces himself that maybe two hundred feet below he can see the top of the elevator. And at the bottom, there's light leaking into the shaft. They stand back. There are times when Dart's emotions need to find a place to sit and wait because they know his focus has returned and he has no mental cycles to spare. A calm descends on him. What triggers it, Dart doesn't know, but he knows when it's happening.

"How far is the bottom from where we'll find Kaira?"

"I don't know where she is, but if she's being held against her will, she'll probably be in jail row."

"How far?"

"Assuming the shaft comes out where I think it does—and it's only a guess—I'd say a brisk fifteen-minute walk."

"Okay. Max, stay here." He hands her the flashlight. "In twenty minutes I want you to fuck up this switchgear. Put a few rounds in it, take a rock to it, drag out wiring. Then accel the hell out of here."

"You don't know where she is, Dart. It's too big a risk, and maybe for nothing," Max says, but more out of duty than the realistic hope of slowing Dart down.

"How's that gonna work?" Scarecrow is agitated. "If we go down there with one accelerator, and you're grabbing the Prasad girl, how do three of us get out? The deal is I go with you. That's the deal."

"I know what the deal is," Dart hisses. "Three of us will fit just fine inside a blast radius. Done it before."

"And also," Max adds, "the deal is that I blow your fucking head off if you don't do what you're told." Dart nods a *thank you* for that reminder. "So when I disable it, I'm guessing there'll be an explosion of alarms. What if you've not found her?"

"What if? Then we resort to Plan B."

"Which is ...?"

"I'll come up with that on my way down."

Max walks up to Dart and digs a fingertip into his chest. "No. Here's Plan B. If she isn't exactly where strawhead here thinks she is, you accel right out of there. We've more than fulfilled the mission. We've found the way in, and when there's a real plan, we'll come back, rescue the precious Kaira, and do whatever else needs to get done. You get that?"

"I get that," he echoes.

"You're an idiot, Darty."

The idea of a farewell kiss flashes across his mind, but it'd likely mean a broken rib too.

FORTY-TWO

The wait for the next mission is unbearable. They could hardly go to Te Wiata and tell him they're ready for a new challenge; anything to serve the Movement. That might look suspicious. So Freya and Sarah sit in their tents, whispering the plan back and forth, looking for flaws. The plan could go right in only one way but wrong in so many ways that Freya had stopped counting. One spectacular failure scenario involves body parts piled in one location with a complementary set in another. But, notwithstanding all the risks, not trying is not an option. This is the only logic that makes the plan a good idea.

Freya and Sarah listen to the loud sex coming from half a dozen tents away. It's no surprise that this was a popular way to pass the day, but what impressed Freya about that particular tent was the sustained level of decibels and its clock-setting regularity. Freya and Sarah just sit and listen for a while, having long ago exhausted the jokes.

"What do you miss most?" Sarah asks.

Freya considers it. "It's corny, but ... my mom."

Sarah smiles. "What's she like?"

"About your age," Freya replies. Sarah grins and gently punches Freya's shoulder. "I'd call her every couple of days, not that I could tell her much about my work. Miss that. She's the reason for where I am. Well, not right now. And all the men in my life weren't worth much of a shit. But I really bucked the trend with Red, right?" Sarah smiles. "She always wanted me to be a scientist. Think she once saw a show or read a book about Jewel Plummer Cobb, the cancer researcher. And then that was it. Little Freya Beaufort was going to be a scientist, come hell or high water. Scary woman, actually. Just the right amount of crazy. Saying *no* to her was never a wise option." Freya sighs. "She'd have some ideas for me about all of this. I'd put her up against Te Wiata any day."

Sarah is about to say something when they notice the shadow on the tent wall.

The flap is pulled back and the sitcom secretary ducks her head in, the tent flap resting on her ginger bouffant. Her lips are crimson and glossy, any flaws in her skin buried deep under strata of powder and paste. She delivers her instructions in a monotone, and without waiting for questions ducks back out.

The mission had been a long time coming, but is still a surprise when it does. Freya and Sarah exchange a look of bemusement, which mutates to one of *are we really going to do this?* Sarah kneels and slides the box from under the bed, opens it and takes out the accelerator. Freya stares at it for a moment, takes one deep breath, and stuffs it into a cloth sack.

They stride with purpose along the rocky corridors, passing Allfours in ones and twos. *How do I go about looking completely innocent? What does that look like? Is it better to keep your eyes down, or to look straight at them as if they're the ones who look suspicious?*

"Here's a joke. Laugh at it," Sarah says. Freya affects a giggle. "Keep laughing."

"It wasn't that funny."

"Then that's your fault." Banter gets them to the door and from within they hear thudding music. The security cam adjusts position and the door slides open. As they step inside, Kaira grabs Freya and hugs her tightly, pinning her arms to her sides. They form a huddle.

"How do I look?" Kaira whispers.

"Perfect. You pull it off." Makeup has lightened Kaira's face by several shades, her hair is tucked under a baseball cap, and she's wearing a plaid shirt with jeans. She's Sarah.

"Thanks. I was worried I couldn't carry off this much style."

"Fuck off," Sarah says. They clasp each other's hands and squeeze, then they break the huddle. Freya and Kaira promptly exit and make their way towards the transport cavern. They pass not a single Allfour en route to the transport cave, and Freya realizes that the most critical part of the plan had always been to have tremendous luck.

The cavern is empty. This has been the pattern for missions that didn't require weapons to be handed over. They wait. *Is this too long? It seems too long.* Sarah was supposed to wait for five minutes and then follow. So where is she?

Finally the door opens and Sarah walks in, cloth sack in hand. Freya grabs Kaira, bending to kiss her cheek, and holds her tight. Sarah nods and Freya takes a deep breath. "Ready."

Wherever Te Wiata's accelerators had taken them, the ambient light and temperature are about the same as their point of departure: gloomy and cold. Freya releases Kaira, looking her up and down to check she's intact. Around the small room are portraits of bearded men in ruffs and long-nosed women in bonnets, all staring indignantly at the new arrivals. The furniture is plush and ornate, and one entire wall is a tapestry of a nobleman sitting with confident superiority atop a horse. It all has a Tudor feel to Freya, although that's a random guess. Sarah hands the cloth sack to Freya.

"Me? Why me?" She realizes that for all their planning,

they hadn't decided who'd wear the accelerator.

"It has to be you," Sarah says. "It's been too long for me. Can't risk screwing it up."

"Shit." Freya lifts her sleeve to strap it on.

"Other arm," Sarah says.

Freya nods. Two accelerators on one arm is probably bad practice. Once it's secured to her wrist with the chemical pods resting on her forearm, she starts to program it, just then realizing she has to do it upside down. So that's infinity plus one failure scenarios for this plan. And the biggest, nastiest possible failure is coming up. Three adults, one accelerator—a perfect recipe for short-charging themselves. She touches the accelerator screen, which comes to life, and then punches in the coordinates she's memorized. Pivoting her elbow to get a view that's almost the right way up, she checks her input once, twice, three times.

"For fuck's sake," Kaira says.

Freya pulls them in tight, both women a head shorter than her. She loops her arms around their necks, and her finger hovers above the *Activate* key. She closes her eyes tight and presses the screen.

Through her eyelids she detects that the gloom has been replaced by bright light. "You okay?" Both heads nod beneath her chin. She releases her grip and they all look around.

Something is wrong. This is still the Tudor room although now it's suddenly well-lit. She had screwed up the programming. But ...? They look at each other, perplexed by what had and had not just happened.

Just then a door bursts open and in walk two people followed by a third—Barry Te Wiata. Freya can't assemble any mental model of what had just happened. Te Wiata seems like a giant in a toy house as he stands there, arms crossed and glaring at Freya. The sitcom secretary roughly undoes the good accelerator from Freya's arm and hands it to the man in the suit and tie. Freya remembers him from her first close encounter with Te Wiata. The man inspects the accelerator then says, "Risley, 2025." Freya gets the impression that bad news has just been delivered.

Te Wiata shakes his head. "You manage to rescue the granddaughter of the great man himself and the place you choose to take her is Risley?" Freya has no idea what this means or what's happening. "The intellectual caliber of TMAers never ceases to amaze me," he says.

Freya ignores this. "So you two found each other," she says to the secretary and the banker. "Some things are meant to be."

The secretary glares at her with fresh loathing.

"But the boundless stupidity of TMA is really a mixed blessing," Te Wiata continues. "It can work for us and it can work against us. On the one hand, it makes you gullible enough to think you could really rescue my dear friend's granddaughter so easily." Freya's stomach tightens. "I mean, really. You thought you could just waft in and then stroll out with her? And using an accelerator that somehow your partner had held on to? Seriously, Freya?"

Sarah leaves Freya's side to stand behind Te Wiata.

Freya maintains calm as she feels her stomach plummet. "Well," she says, "what a little bitch *you* turned out to be."

Sarah strides calmly past Te Wiata and delivers a hard slap to Freya's cheek. Freya gasps despite herself.

"Now now, Sarah, no need for that," Te Wiata says. He turns back to Freya. "It's her hot Italian blood. Anyway, as I was saying, TMA's stupidity can work against us, too. You see, I couldn't have made it any easier for them to locate us here. Time and again they've been given the opportunity to track us down. It'd just take a rigged accelerator and a little tachyonic decryption technology. You'd think they could have worked that out. But no."

"And why would you want them to track you down?" Freya asks.

"If I told you, that should concern you, shouldn't it?" Te Wiata grins. "Unless dear Sarah gets to you first, of course." He chuckles. Sarah is stony-faced: no shame, no anger, not even a note of self-satisfaction. "So I'm going to tell you. The reason I want them to track me down is so that I can track *them* down."

"You know where they are," Freya says. Te Wiata surveys her carefully.

"Hmm. I suppose it is possible you have no idea. I could believe you're just a TMA peon. Or maybe you really did join the Movement and you just don't know. You see, they have a base. Not the ramshackle collection of huts in Risley but a base where their valuable people work—their slightly less stupid people. I have good reason to believe that one of them is your friend's grandfather. And I have to give it to them: they do have that place well-hidden."

Freya turns to look at Kaira who stares back with incredulity.

"If they get someone here who's dumb enough to 'liberate' an Allfour, then we'll track exactly where they go. And when the Allfour being liberated is Kaira Prasad herself, well then surely the only safe location for her is their very secret place. With granddad." Te Wiata sighs. "That was the plan at least, but as I said, it calls for some measure of intellect on the part of the TMA. So it was a rather flawed plan, I now see."

"Yes, flawed it was," Freya says. "But TMA comes out on top because you're standing there with your thumb up your ass and the TMA base is still hidden. No?" Freya doesn't know where these words came from but is enjoying the discomfort on the faces of the banker and his secretary. This is the belligerence that had tended to help her career, although now she sees its possible downside.

Te Wiata frowns. "I admit I make mistakes, Freya. But I learn from them. I see now that I need to replace that plan with one that relies on TMA's stupidity and not their wit. *That* plan will work."

"So I wasn't litmus," Kaira says in a near whisper, the full realization washing over her. "I was bait."

"Oh, you make your old Uncle Barry sad. It's a delight

to have you close, whatever the other benefits."

"But why?" Kaira asks. "Why do you want to get to my grandfather? He did everything to help you. Where do you think you'd be without him? Without everything happening exactly the way it did?"

"Well, that's what we'll find out, Kaira." He smiles warmly.

Kaira's eyes widen. "That's the Big One, isn't it?" she says. "The Big One is doing something to my grandfather. Killing him? The ultimate victory against TMA? The Big One was all about Barry Te Wiata and nothing else." Freya looks back and forth between Kaira and Te Wiata. Is he that crazy? There are a thousand reasons—

"How insane *are* you, Barry?" Kaira asks. "Do you really think—"

"Please, Kaira. We're family. I won't allow this business to get between us." Freya and Kaira shoot an incredulous look at each other. "And there's so much you don't understand, that you don't know. I don't want my beautiful Kaira worrying about all of that."

Patronizing fat prick.

"Anyway, enough of this."

Adrenaline courses through Freya's body. This is it. This is where it ends for her. She grabs Kaira's hand and squeezes it tightly. Then, in the periphery of her vision, she catches someone else walking into the Tudor room. She turns and Red smiles at her.

"Of course," she says.

Te Wiata shakes his head. "I can see why you'd be a little paranoid at this point, Freya," he says, "but I've decided your friend, Athos, deserves a second chance, so I've asked him to take care of you for a while. And Kaira, let's get you somewhere safe."

The sitcom secretary unclasps Kaira and Freya's grip, her reinforced crimson nails digging into flesh. Kaira looks back at Freya as she's being dragged from the Tudor room.

FORTY-THREE

Freya follows Red in silence. At least she's not dead: not short-charged, shot, or strangled. That's a silver lining. After a few turns, she realizes where they're heading. Of course. That sends a message. *You're of no concern to me, Freya Beaufort. You just don't have the wherewithal to be even a minor threat, so you're going right back to the dorm to live out a life with the partner you deserve—Athos the imbecile.* In its way, this is crueler than sweet death.

Red lifts the tent flap. "It's good to be back," he says. Sarah's tent is gone, although the cot is still there.

"I'm not getting in there with you," Freya says.

Red sighs. "I swear, I had nothing to do with it."

"Nothing to do with what? Staging the escape or landing us in this hell in the first place?"

Red frowns. "Okay, I did work with Barry to get you here. I admit that. But I didn't think it'd work out this way. I just wanted us all to be at the heart of the Movement. To be with the man himself. I thought the Musketeers deserved to be on center stage."

Freya shakes her head. "Center stage? Center stage of a gothic horror."

Red looks down, unprepared to meet Freya's glare.

"Maybe I wouldn't do it the same way again."

She stares at his pathetic figure. Is this just more play-acting? Is it possible he really is that dumb and naive? But the answer doesn't matter. Either way, Te Wiata had picked the severest form of punishment he could by thrusting her back together with this sad creature.

"You take the tent." He's barely audible. "I'll use Sarah's old cot." Freya looks at the cot from under which Sarah had produced the dummy accelerator. She can at least enjoy the fact that Te Wiata saw this escape fiasco as a failed mission—Sarah's failed mission. Freya hopes that the consequences for her are brutal. That thought is her only pleasure.

Fear of Te Wiata's wrath is overtaken by stultifying boredom. Freya sits on her cot each day, the only excursions from her tent being to eat or shower. Red is smart enough not to bother her. She rarely sees him, and she has no idea where he goes each day. She's happy about that since the thought of him just sitting out there on the edge of Sarah's cot, waiting for her to come out, is horrendous. Maybe Te Wiata is sending him out on missions. Maybe by this point, Te Wiata does it for his own amusement, and if Red is killed then that's icing.

And she thinks about Kaira—where she is and what she's doing. She hopes that at least her fellow Musketeer had been brought back to her plush apartment. She wakes each day to thoughts of Kaira. And they stay until she sleeps. She imagines Kaira lying beside her in the dark of her tent, both of them plotting an escape that can't fail. She feels Kaira's hand on her cheek as she whispers the plot into her ear, lips brushing her earlobe.

She had sucked down a meal requiring no teeth. The vending machine had puked it out and she had spooned it up. She had been getting a lot of attention and everyone had looked at her for just a moment too long. Was it contempt for the betrayal? Or was it stark admiration for what she had attempted? Maybe it was neither. Maybe no one even knows what happened. She didn't care.

She makes her way back to the chaotic refugee camp. As she negotiates the obstacle course to her tent, something gets her attention. At first, she doesn't know why. It's the guy with the wispy yellow hair who dresses as a medieval peasant. But she'd seen this weirdo navigating the dorm plenty of times, so what seems different? She realizes he's not alone this time. That's not usual. And the person with him ... There's something ... It's not his face. His face is hidden behind a bushy, brown beard. And he's not in especially strange clothing by the standards of this place—it's a peasant getup. No, it's his gait. Graceful and fluid, like a panther, as if he's gliding from the waist up with no evidence of taking strides. Why is that familiar? Where has she—

Fuck. That's the Musketeer. That's Dart. Kaira's Dart.

Freya takes a step back and collides with something.

A grizzled old guy on a stool mutters something as he inspects the coffee spillage on his shirt.

"Sorry," she says, "I wasn't ..." When she looks back up they're gone. She takes off towards where they had been, oblivious to the low-lying obstacles in her path. She'd lost them amidst the hubbub of the camp: a riot of color and activity and clamor. Someone is saying something to her, but it blends with the ambient hum.

"Hey," she hears from behind. "You just walked over my stuff." The pitch is high and penetrating.

"Sorry," Freya says without turning. A hand lands heavily on her shoulder and spins her around. She's facing a clean-shaven, frog-eyed man with blond hair, radiating indignance. Freya looks at him for a moment and then brings her forehead down hard onto the bridge of his nose. He staggers backwards and raises a hand to shield his face.

"Mad cow," he shouts.

Freya turns and keeps walking. "Moo."

Had Dart always been here? Did he break in somehow? That seems unlikely. This'll make Kaira happy. And Kaira being happy would make her happy, too. Yet ... There is no 'yet'. But how could she get the good news to Kaira? How could she see Kaira's face when she's told? That's what's making Freya sad. She sees that now. That must be it.

FORTY-FOUR

It's a long way down, each step echoing in the shaft, but at least Dart has a ladder to clutch. No one would call his plan an airtight one. But each rung gets Dart a step closer to Kaira. He looks up but can't see Max, only the blinding flashlight. Someone might choose this very moment to use the elevator. Dart wonders why he always has to think this way, but it's likely what's kept him alive. Optimists probably die much younger than pessimists, although they're sure to see the upside to their predicament right up until the very end.

It's a deeper descent than it had seemed from the top, but now they are close to the source of light at the bottom of the shaft. "Wait," he says in a stage whisper. Although he can't hear voices, he's not going to rule out the possibility that they're about to present themselves in front of a roomful of Allfours. He swings around the edge of the ladder and jumps down into the space between the side of the elevator and the opening. He peeps out and sees a room lined with shelves, floor to ceiling. The shelves are full of electronic components, reels of cable and tools. No sign of people. He steps into the room and Scarecrow follows.

"Is this where you thought we'd be?" Dart asks.

"Can't tell yet." The Allfour in the lead, they exit the supply room and find themselves in a corridor with rock walls and low-hung fluorescent lights. The corridor is long and Dart pushes Scarecrow to pick up the pace.

"You have any clue where we are?" Dart asks. Scarecrow slows to turn around but Dart says, "No, just keep going."

If Max sets off the alarms and they're still lost, then Dart has no plan.

"I thought I'd recognize where we are by now. Maybe I'm a little off." Dart suppresses his first reaction. He's risking everything—his life, maybe Kaira's life—on someone who looks like he's stuffed with hay and should be standing in a field with a wooden pole up his ass. Yet he has no other options.

At the end of the ascending corridor, something metallic comes into view. They're both panting as they arrive at the door. It slides open. What they step into is a cavern that's maybe fifty feet high, with stalactites above and water cascading down the far wall, draining to somewhere beneath a pile of rocks. Scarecrow says, "C'mon," and Dart senses relief in the Allfour. They cross the cavern where another door opens itself and Dart steps into ... a mess hall? It has the acoustics of a large cafeteria: the clatter of cutlery and the indistinct rumble of a hundred conversations. He keeps his eyes down as he follows the Allfour across the cafeteria floor. Surely someone here must have witnessed him confronting Te Wiata in Glasgow. Was Dart crazy to think that a beard is all it would take to disguise himself—like Clark Kent with his pair of glasses?

They enter an even larger cavern strewn with tents of all shapes and colors. Allfours are navigating between them or collecting in groups for conversation. What are the odds that absolutely none of them had been in Glasgow? Scarecrow is wending briskly through the randomly placed tents along a path he seems to have navigated many times before. Does Joad know just how many people are holed up in Te Wiata's bunker? This space alone contains hundreds—as many, maybe even more, than Tomatotown.

They reach the far side of the camp and Scarecrow starts to ascend a staircase. Dart follows until they're standing on a balcony overlooking the camp. Two men survey Dart, but Scarecrow says something that causes them to lose interest. They enter yet another corridor and accelerate to a jog. He has lost track of time and braces for the alarm to sound at any minute. It'd be game over. This corridor continually branches, but the Allfour seems to know where he's going.

After another few minutes of navigating the maze, the corridor turns sharply to the right and Scarecrow signals for Dart to halt. His back to the wall, Scarecrow peeks around the corner. "This is it. This is jail row," he whispers.

"Where Kaira is?"

"I never said that. I said *maybe*. But there is a guy with a big gun standing outside one of the doors." Dart pulls Scarecrow back and takes his place at the corner. The sentry is too far away for an accurate shot. Yet walking any closer seems like a recipe for getting shredded.

"Come on," Scarecrow says, walking past Dart. "Hey," he calls. The guard turns his weapon on them.

"Stay back," the guard yells. Scarecrow continues undaunted, Dart close behind with a hand on the pistol tucked into the back of his belt.

"I'm not staying back. Message from Barry."

"Stay back," the guard repeats, this time more urgently. "What message?"

"I'm not going to bellow it up the corridor, soldier."

The guard keeps his rifle trained on them as they walk toward him. Dart can see rapid calculations occurring behind the squat guard's small, bright eyes.

"It's about the Prasad woman," Dart says. The guard is too late to suppress his nod. She's in there. "We need to go in."

"Not a chance. No one goes in there without authorization."

"Is that right? And Barry's authorization is no good

here?" Scarecrow says.

"I don't—"

The feeling of an ice pick pierces Dart's ear drums. It takes an instant to register that it's the alarm—and it's the loudest, sharpest, most penetrative sound he has ever heard. With the acoustics of the cave, it feels like it could do more human damage than anything that'd set it off. It's in that instant that the guard flinches, and with the agility that had kept Dart alive through a hundred lunatic Allfour missions, he lifts the barrel of the rifle with one hand and pulls the pistol from his belt with the other, pressing it into the guard's forehead.

"Take it off," Dart shouts above the din. The guard pulls the gun strap over his head and hands the weapon to Dart. "Now punch in the code." Dart tilts his head at the keypad next to the metal door.

"I don't know the entry code," the guard shouts.

"Well then, you're no use to me," Dart says, raising the pistol to the guard's head.

"Okay, okay." He turns and prods the keypad. The door doesn't move. "Sorry, no." He makes a second attempt and this time the door slides open. Dart steps inside. It's dark but as his eyes acclimatize he sees a silhouette in the gloom.

"Kaira?" There's no response. "Kaira?"

The shadow approaches and enters the light from the corridor. He sees the delicate features of her face, and eyes that had been squinting in the light now open to reveal the large, dark orbs he knew. The alarm stops and his ears whistle. He moves towards her.

Scarecrow is shouting from behind. "He's getting away."

"We'll be long gone," Dart says. He turns just in time to receive Kaira's lips on his. The rifle clatters to the ground and he slips the pistol back into his belt, freeing his arms to wrap around her.

"Where have you been?" Kaira asks. As the perfume he had forgotten fills his senses, he barely notices the gun being pulled from his belt. Scarecrow is pointing it at him.

"We're leaving her here. You can come back to get her, but I haven't come this far to get ripped apart by a tachyon blast."

"I told you," Dart says. "Three of us is no problem. I've done—"

"Why should I take the risk?"

"Who's he?" Kaira asks.

"He speaks Anglo-Saxon."

"Why is that useful?"

"You're in eighth century England. I guess you wouldn't know that."

"Come to think of it," the Allfour says, "take off the accelerator. I don't need you either."

"And where do you think you'd go? You'll need TMA protection wherever you wind up."

"TMA protection?" Scarecrow spits back. "You're hilarious. They couldn't even protect *her*. Now, take it off."

Scarecrow's body blossoms into petals of red with the staccato of rapid gunfire. The squat guard is in the doorway and now turns his weapon on Dart.

"About fucking time," Kaira shouts. She stoops to pick up the pistol next to the bloody mass that had been the Allfour. "Get me back to Barry, right now."

"Leave the gun where it is," the guard shouts.

"But I need it to do this," she says. A dark hole appears in the guard's forehead and he falls backwards. Dart grabs Kaira and rolls up his sleeve. She looks at the accelerator and shakes her head urgently. "No, you can't accelerate."

"That's what you think."

FORTY-FIVE

Freya slaps the palms of her hands onto her ears. There has to be some intensity of noise that's unhearable because your eardrums have already ruptured, and she thought it'd be well below this. She pushes her head out of the tent flap, not daring to remove her hands from her ears. The camp is alive with painful bewilderment. Red is sitting on his cot and he shakes his head at her. The agony lasts for a full minute.

"What the hell—" Freya begins.

"Unbelievable," Red says. With the alarm silenced, Freya hears the frantic chatter, but there's no sign of any mobilization. "Must be something pretty serious."

"You think?" Freya replies. "I thought maybe your fucking microwave dinner was ready." Red smiles and he looks like someone else, like a person she knew in a different place.

It dawns on her. Was her sighting of the skinny Musketeer related to the alarm from hell going off? Did he get caught? Did he try to break out? With Kaira? Did they succeed? When it comes to speculation, it's usually none of the above. She re-enters her tent, knowing that no one is going to figure out what's going on any time soon. And when they do, she'll hear about it from a hundred directions.

Freya is on her way to her tent when she hears the commotion. It's a woman in distress. Then she hears a male voice. Disturbances are commonplace in the cave, but this one gets her attention: she recognizes one of the voices. It's Red.

Freya gets closer. The woman is stooped and sobbing, and Red has an arm around her shoulder. *What has the asshole done now?* The distraught woman has a headful of thick, brown curls, some of them stuck to her round, cherubic face, which is red and tearstained. She pushes Red away. "No, I'm going. I'm not staying here. I'm going."

Red moves in again to put an arm around her but she pushes him off. He looks up nervously towards the observation balcony. "We'll all be out of here soon enough," he says with metered calm. "Don't try to leave this way. It's not what you think."

"No. They said I can leave if I want to," she says, her words punctuated by sobs. By now they have drawn an audience that's watching in silence. "They said it's okay. It's my choice. And I'm choosing this. Now. I'm leaving."

A man and woman with the size and supercilious confidence typical of Te Wiata's people have pushed their way through the gathering crowd. They walk off with the distressed woman, clearing a path through the assembled crowd. Anxious looks are exchanged for a few seconds before the crowd disperses in silence.

The lights are dimmed so it's to be taken as nighttime. After the commotion of the alarm earlier, Freya can't sleep and decides a walk might settle her. As always, day and night, Red is sitting on his cot. He looks up, surprised to see her at this hour, whatever hour that is. This time, she doesn't turn away.

"I've fucked everything up, haven't I?" he says. "You,

Kaira, me. What the hell have I done?"

"If you want a debate, Red, you better pick a different topic."

His lips twitch a smile but he looks down, uncomfortable with Freya's stare.

"What can I do? There's nothing, is there? And if there were, I'd screw it up and makes things worse."

Freya can think of nothing to say. She could lacerate him or she could comfort him, but neither seems worthwhile. He's broken and done for. She could ask him if he knows anything about Dart being here, but she doesn't. If he'd known about Dart, he would have said something, and at worst, she'd be giving something away. Still, she doesn't want to leave him quite yet. Why, she doesn't know. Maybe it's something to do with Risley and a distant memory of the man she'd once took him to be. Though, in fairness, she had let go of that man only weeks after they'd hooked up. Or maybe it's because she's had no human companionship for too long, and at least he's still broadly human.

"My ears still haven't recovered," she says. He seems nonplussed. "The alarm—what decibel level do you think? Two hundred?"

"Battle of Cremona," he murmurs, more to himself than to Freya. That party trick seems a lifetime ago. She sits on the cot beside him and for a while they just stare at their feet. "Did a lot of walking around the base, just soul searching."

"Did you find one?"

He shakes his head. "I hope one day you won't be so angry at me."

Red turns to her and smiles as if a new mood has descended on him. "You know, believe it or not, I used to be quite smart. Always top of my class. Kid most likely to succeed. In my PhD program, no one could touch me. But then I arrive at TMA, where everyone was top of their class, and it doesn't take long to figure out that I'm not top-shelf—nowhere near it—and that I'm going nowhere in that organization. I'm no Prasad, no Galois, no Geller, no you, Slayer."

"Don't feel so bad. You're part of the rich tapestry of humanity we call the bell curve."

He flashes a grin. "I thought maybe the Movement could be a fresh start for me. Maybe in the Movement I could be something. And we did have such a great life, Freya. The Musketeers. We had a cause and we had adventures. And I brought you onboard because I wanted you to be part of it. I wanted you and me to be doing it together." He shivers. "And then Posh appears, so innocently. Just another dumb Allfours band with stupid names."

"Yeah, so innocent back then. Only killing people out of a sense of mischief."

"But we killed the right people, Freya. Bad people. Dart made sure of that. He never bought into the net moral neutrality bullshit for a minute. He made sure we did good. I know I played the asshole—the purist for the cause—but I knew Dart was always right. We all did. He made the decisions." Red shakes his head. "But then *I* made a decision. Yeah, I could make decisions, too." He looks at Freya. "And here we are."

Freya is about to place a comforting hand on Red's back but catches herself. "You tried to save that woman. I saw it. Maybe there's a part of you that isn't pure shit."

No smile. If he'd heard Freya, he doesn't acknowledge it.

Outside, it sounds different this morning. The chatter in the dorm is more hushed, less mirthful. The camp had been growing, or at least getting more densely packed in its haphazard design, and with it had come the ever-increasing volume of prattle. And the mood of the chatter had been slowly changing. Levity had been on the uptick as if they were seeing light on the horizon.

But today, the talk is muted. Freya ducks out of her tent

and there's a cluster of Allfours around it. They're all staring up at one of the balconies at a line of several figures. It's the sitcom banker and his secretary, the tall, lean guy with the face full of acne she'd seen in Te Wiata's office, and bracketing them are two familiar strong-armers. There's a gap in the middle of the line—a two-person, Te Wiata-shaped gap. Red is standing in front of her and she asks him what's happening. He shrugs. After a few minutes of what Freya assumes is anticipation-building, Te Wiata takes his place.

"Good morning, Allfours." His voice is amplified. This is new. "It's gratifying to stand here and look at so many of you who have dedicated yourselves to our cause—to the Movement. The first thing I want to do is thank you. Thank you for not flinching in your commitment." Red takes a step back to be beside Freya. "You're on the right side of history. You know it because you're the designers of history."

What the fuck is he talking about?

"We know that we all have an inalienable right to the freedom of movement, in *any* dimension. We are Allfours." This gets a cheer.

What assholes.

He continues, "What nature has given us, no one takes away. Not any government, not any junta, not any army, not any church, and certainly not the TMA."

There's another cheer, this time louder.

Most of these people were once TMA. They were the cream of the scientific cream. How can she reconcile that with this crowd, so fucking naive? But maybe at this point, anything that portends change is something to be cheered.

"The other thing I want to thank you for is your patience. I know you've been kept in the dark on a lot of things. Like why we're here and what we've been waiting for. And I know some of you filled in the gaps with your own theories." He nods, smiling at his observation, and nervous laughter breaks out.

Toady little shits.

"Oh, yes. The Big One has been many things to many people. I wouldn't be surprised if some of you were beginning to think there is no Big One." The sitcom secretary smirks, making clear to anyone who isn't mesmerized by Te Wiata that she was not among the doubters. "Don't deny it. But others of you have kept the faith. You knew that you'd be informed when the time was right." Te Wiata slowly and dramatically surveys his rapt audience, continuing to nod in affirmation of himself, then says, "And today the time is right."

Silence descends on the camp.

FORTY-SIX

"Don't accelerate," Kaira shouts.

In a room flooded with sunlight, Dart sees Max and Hay who both have that *deer in the headlights* look of exiting an acceleration. Kaira pushes Dart away, frantic to get the device off her wrist. "Take this off me. Right now." She's hyperventilating. "They'll accel me back."

"No, Kaira. We're inside a shield," Dart says. "We're safe."

She begins to control her breathing and surveys the strangers in the room. Max is inspecting her with detached curiosity and Joad is smiling. They had likely acceled back to a point seconds after they had departed from the Tomato facility, or at least that was common practice. It was always revealing to watch a traveler vanish and then instantly reappear with the wear and tear of a long journey. It gave an immediate report on the trip.

"Hello, Kaira," Joad says. "We once met. Long time ago." Kaira looks at him for a moment and then turns to Dart.

"They're tracking me." She shakes her accelerator arm. "This is relaying location data back to them."

"Will the shield prevent that?" Max asks Joad.

Joad's smile disappears. "No. If that's emitting a signal, the nanosecond gap in the shield you just entered through was more than enough to let it transmit. If that thing really is tracking ... we need to assume they've located us."

Dart looks at his father. "That's—"

"Bad," Joad says. "But we got you all back. That's good. Plus Kaira." Max isn't ready yet for the conversation about Kaira.

"I tried to tell you, Dart," Kaira says. "I told you not to accelerate."

Dart shrugs. "I didn't understand. Besides, our options were pretty limited."

Kaira takes Dart's hand and squeezes it. "Did I thank you?"

"You're welcome. All for one, and all that, right?" He hears Max's expletive from behind.

"Te Wiata had a plan," Kaira says, beginning to take in her surroundings. "He'd been waiting for someone to charge in on a rescue mission. That's the way he was going to find ... this place, I assume." She walks over to the plate-glass wall and looks out over the lake and woods. "Is that a tomato?"

"So he *wanted* us to get her out?" Max asks, glancing at Kaira with no affection.

"Did it seem suspiciously easy?" Joad asks.

"Are you fucking kidding me?" Max says.

"No, it didn't seem suspiciously easy," Dart replies.

"Okay," Joad says. "Bottom line is, they've probably located us. Implications? Not good. A lot hinges on us being well-hidden. If Te Wiata gets to us here, he gets a lot closer to his Big One. A lot closer. So I think we can anticipate being visited."

Dart observes his father's calm. He wants to be that way.

"Good news is," Joad continues, "there's no sign that it's happened yet. No tachyon bow waves. No arrivals. No obvious shifts in the timeline. So maybe we have time to think."

Dart awakens before Kaira. She doesn't look damaged or worn—no signs of what she'd been through. As her breasts gently rise and fall, her expression is untroubled, serene. He loves her. He knows that. This is the first time he has felt intact in a long while. Without her, he's someone else—all the worst parts of himself. Yet now he sees the real Kaira, not the memory he'd been clinging to. It's the woman who was always closer to the Allfours' cause than he had ever known how to be. The woman who did what it took. The woman who had calmly put a bullet into an Allfour's head a few hours earlier.

Her eyes flutter open.

"You looking at me?" She smiles.

Dart nods. "Get used to it," he whispers and kisses her.

"We're on high alert," Joad tells Dart as they look out over the lake. "Any tachyonic signals, even ones likely to be noise, are being analyzed and pinpointed. Max is leading the field trips, when needed. She insisted."

"She's on a guilt trip," Dart says.

"Oh, do you think, Casy?"

"Don't be hard on her. It was all my doing. I made her do it."

"*Made* her do it? A TMA operative and you *made* her do it?"

"Yes. And you know, I hear some crazy-ass legends about the great Joad Bevan and what he made happen to get his ladylove out of the shit."

Joad looks at the sky. There's a big flyer in the distance, probably out over the sea rather than crossing the island.

"Are you seeing activity?" Dart asks.

"We're seeing bow waves. A few readings that could actually be transportation waves, but if anything or anyone has arrived, we haven't found them."

"What do you think he intends—Te Wiata?"

"The most valuable thing we have here is Prasad. I'm guessing he's figured that out. He just didn't know where to find us."

"Until now."

"Until now." Joad gives his son a resigned smile, then asks as a *by the way*, "Are you sure about Kaira? Are we at risk?"

Dart is no position to follow through on his first instinct of angry indignation, so he says, "No, I'm sure."

"I mean, we need her to be here either way," Joad says. "Having Prasad's granddaughter out there was a big vulnerability." He places a hand on Dart's shoulder and squeezes. "You behaved like an irresponsible asshole, Casy, but I guess that's how I know you're really my son. You pulled off one hell of a mission, even though it was the wrong mission."

"I'm afraid that's as good as it gets with your kid, Joad."

FORTY-SEVEN

Daylight had been switched on early and mobilization is underway. Freya and Red watch as the camp thins out, Allfours exiting in every direction. Somehow, everyone seems to know what to do and when, although neither Freya nor Red are in the loop.

A big oaf in plaid walks up to Freya. "C'mon," he says and then points at Red. "You, too."

It's the route to Te Wiata's office, and they are walking against a current of Allfours. They enter. Everyone inside is wearing military camouflage fatigues.

"Look at all the little toy soldiers," Freya says and giggles.

Te Wiata smirks at his large, acned lieutenant, by now used to Freya's style. The sitcom secretary and Sarah glare at her and she wonders which of them despises her more. "Those raspberry nails are going to stand out in the jungle," she says.

"I have a surprise for you, Dr. Freya," Te Wiata says. "You're coming with us."

This does not look like happy news for the secretary who, Freya suspects, assumed her boss was summoning them to receive a bullet each. "Both of you are coming, in fact."

"So we'll all be part of the Big One," Freya says, with extra contempt applied to the last two words. "The epic battle between good and evil, right and wrong, freedom and tyranny, heroes and villains. And you're all dressed up for it, like little soldiers." Freya knew she had been too long-winded to cut deep.

"Freya, have a care for yourself," Te Wiata says. "Make no mistake; this battle will be all those things. It'll be decisive, it'll end TMA's hegemony, end their existence, in fact, and it'll shift the timeline in a seismic way. This *is* the Big One. It'll end the war, and no one will be in doubt of who has won."

"Are you serious?" Freya asks. "End the war? You, the victors? First, there is no war. And your army is just a bunch of overeducated morons up to pranks and homicidal hijinks."

Sarah takes a step towards Freya. "No," Te Wiata says. "That's okay. She has an opinion and I respect that. Were you always TMA, Freya? Always a spy in our midst?"

Red is about to protest but she raises her hand to stop him.

"I was never a lunatic who thinks the only cause worth fighting for is putting Barry Te Wiata on a throne. That no price is too high." She shakes her head slowly, pausing to let her next words hit home. "You're no Allfour, Te Wiata. You're just riding them like the dumb beasts they are."

"I'm no Allfour? My, and you say *I'm* the lunatic. Anyway, we must move on. I really don't care what you are and who you're with. It makes no difference now. What's important is that you and my lovely Kaira have a strong affection for one another."

"A pair of dykes," Sarah says, a savage grin spreading across her face. She looks at Red who is just looking back dumbly.

"Oh really, Sarah," Te Wiata says. "Sometimes I worry about you."

"You can see why she'd turn to it," Sarah says, glaring at

Red. The secretary's grin creases her entire face.

"Now stop that," Te Wiata says without conviction. "The point is that dear Freya may be of value to us. Maybe she'll turn out to be just what we need." He nods at Freya. "And maybe she won't. Still, I want to be sure we're using every arrow in our quiver. So you're coming with us. You get to see the Big One firsthand. What tales you'll be able to tell. Well, if you survive, that is."

With this, Te Wiata walks to the door. Then, as an afterthought, he approaches Red. His meaty fist crunches down hard onto Red's cheekbone, driving the Musketeer down onto his knees.

"You brought a TMA operative into our midst, Athos."

FORTY-EIGHT

"Casy to ops" blares the PA system. Well, that's new. He exits the library banks and lopes down the corridor to the sunlit foyer, taking the staircase three steps at a time.

"The resolution isn't great but I'd say about three hundred," Dart hears as he enters the operations center. Joad is looking over the shoulder of the seated man, and in front of them is a wall monitor displaying a map of the island, a seemingly random distribution of flashing green lights spread across it. The ops center is small and unimpressive compared to Risley, although the technology likely only needs the four operators lined up behind their consoles.

"Three hundred accel events?" Dart asks.

"Arrivals," Joad says as more green dots appear on the screen.

"Three fifty," the operators says.

"Okay, get me the west campus shift director."

The wait is long enough for Joad to start pacing.

"Joon here."

"Joon, we're entering Protocol 1. Evacuate Prasad."

"Copy that."

More green dots appear around the island, some of them

right up to the boundary of the shield.

"Yas, we're entering Protocol 3. Accel out the classified vault."

"Will do," says another of the operators.

"You think this is it?" Dart asks.

"It's something," Joad replies.

"I'm having difficulty executing. Let me try again."

Joad waits a few seconds, peering over the operator's shoulder. "We good?"

"No. Can't accel the vault. It's as if the shield isn't opening for us."

"A malfunction?"

The operator's fingers deftly slide across her screen. "Nothing obvious, sir," she says. "No sign of any faults."

"Figure it out fast, Yas."

"It's as if there's an outer shield in place."

"Shit. This is it," Dart whispers to himself. Then the speaker comes to life.

"Joon, here. Protocol 1 is, so far, ineffective. Accel failure."

"Same problem here," Joad replies.

Dart steps forward and places a hand on his father's shoulder. "They've put a shield around the whole island. That's my guess."

Joad looks at his son. "Mine, too."

"So, no reinforcements," Max says.

"And no communications out," Joad adds.

Dart is cycling his fists open and closed. "How many now?"

"Could be as many as five hundred. Some of the tachyon blasts are wide focus. They could be batching in people. And equipment," Joad says.

"Like an interference shield assembly."

Max places a hand on her holstered pistol. "We need to go out there and see what's happening. Green dots don't tell us much. We gotta know if we're looking at a highly armed force of crack troops or a mob of cretinous Allfours holding their dicks and chanting Movement anthems. Maybe it's nothing to do with the Movement." She's looking alternately between Joad and Dart. Dart feels complimented.

"You're right," Joad says after a deliberative pause. "Pick half a dozen of your best and take a look."

"No, I'm not taking a squad with me. Need to be agile. I'll pick one other."

"Me," Dart says, but Max shakes her head. "Yes, me. I got us into this shit. And besides, *we're* a crack team now."

They're in a wooded area running along the bank of the lake between the main campus and the location where a small cluster of incoming had been detected. Dart grips his automatic rifle, which he's almost certain he knows how to use. Distant voices echo hollowly through the trees.

"Keep low," Max whispers. "And unhook your finger from around the trigger for fuck's sake." The idea of this place—TMA's ultimate sanctuary—being overrun by invaders makes Dart queasy. He guesses that means he's back on side. And something has gone badly wrong that's his own doing.

Max waves Dart to drop and they kneel in the long vegetation. Max points ahead to where maybe a dozen of them are gathered. About half are in camouflage and carrying rifles, and a smaller group appear to be from a much earlier era based on their furs, tunics, and breeches. Their faces are barely visible behind long matted hair and beards, and they watch the laughing soldiers, not in on the joke.

"What the hell can be going on there?" Dart whispers.

"They've got the discipline of Allfours," Max whispers back.

"And the guys with the axes and shields?"

Max shrugs. "Could be bolstering their forces with those big bastards."

"Fuck, they look like Vikings."

"Yeah. Seems like the sort of asshole statement Te Wiata might make: *Time is my sandpit.* That sort of thing."

A twig snaps and Max turns. Dart looks around in time to see a camouflaged figure shoot off a single round into the air as Max's burst of gunfire throws him up against a tree. They turn back and the group ahead is looking at them, agape. "Start at the right," she shouts, and Dart brings up his weapon and opens fire. The group falls systematically from the outside in, with looks of bewilderment on their faces rather than fear. Barely a shot had been fired back as far as Dart could tell.

"These poor bastards must have had guns thrust into their hands," Max says. "Okay, now go, go."

They dash through the woods back towards the campus, scanning their surroundings for trouble. Then Dart hears shouting and gunfire. There's motion to their left.

"Keep going," Max shouts. "They couldn't hit a barn."

They burst out of the woods at the same time as the Allfours about a hundred feet away. Now that they're in the open, a line of gunfire cuts into the dirt just ahead. The bursts of gunfire accelerate into a continuous clatter, and Dart feels something cut across the tip of his boot. There's no pain and he doesn't slow down. If they've blown off a toe, he can wait to find out.

Then the volume of gunfire takes off. Ahead is a row of concrete barriers and most of the barrage is coming from behind them. To his left the Allfours are dropping en masse. Suddenly the gunfire stops and there's only the sound of the TMA guards ahead shouting at them, as if they were dawdling. As they hit the barriers, the guards drag them over. Dart drops to his knees, heaving to catch his breath.

Joad looks over his shoulder as Dart and Max enter the ops

center. "You okay?"

"Lost a layer of skin on a big toe, but otherwise, yes."

"They're Allfours," Max says. "No question. Dressed up in fancy fatigues but they have the signature incompetence."

"Up to eight hundred," Joad says looking back at the map. "That's a hell of a lot of Allfours."

"They're not all Allfours," Max says. "We saw others among them. Looked to us like Vikings or something."

Joad is incredulous. "He really is fucking crazy. And he thinks he can control them? I'll bet he sees himself as a new Xerxes with an army mustered from all lands and times."

Dart watches new green lights appear. "No matter how disorganized they are, those are numbers that can cause some damage."

The door bursts open and a thick-set woman in a guard's uniform rushes in. Dart recognizes her as chief of campus security services.

"How many people do we have competent with a weapon?" Joad asks her.

"Including security and operatives, thirty. Maybe an additional ten staff who might not shoot off their own feet."

Max says, "Okay. We need to get them over to the west campus, right now."

"No." Joad shakes his head. "Do that and our main campus staff are undefended. It'll be a massacre."

"And if Prasad is taken, we see the mother of all timeline shifts. That's Mission One—"

"You don't need to remind me of Mission One." Joad hadn't raised his voice, which meant that the irritation cut deep. He turns to the security chief.

"Meg, I'll take five of them and we'll try to get across to the west campus. You stay here and evacuate all staff into the accelerator facility. Should be easier to defend. At least for a while. And we're in Protocol 7. Flame the classified vault."

There's a distant burst of gunfire and the sound of shattering glass. "Dart, get Kaira. Max, you're coming with us."

FORTY-NINE

Freya's wrists are handcuffed in front of her, and each time the line inches forward, Sarah drags her by the arm.

"You really didn't age well, did you, Sarah?" Red says from behind. "You must have waited fifty years before you bailed on TMA. So fucking indecisive." Freya dares only a twitch of a smile.

"You'd be wearing a pair of these bracelets, too, if it was up to me, asshole," Sarah spits back at Red. "A moron's no safer than a traitor." The line leads to a station where weapons are being handed out, and beyond that, an accelerator pad where people are being popped out in batches.

"Are they really giving weapons to these jokers?" Freya says. "They're as likely to shoot each other as an adversary."

"These are real Allfours," Sarah replies. "Not TMA operatives or imbeciles. They know what they're doing because they're the ones who aren't dead."

A scrawny, zit-covered man is handing out assault rifles and pistols and wishing everyone *happy hunting*. His thick-lensed glasses make him look like a puppet with swollen eyes.

"Not him," Sarah says as Red reaches for a rifle. "He's

designated cannon fodder." They take their place on the accelerator pad with about twenty other Allfours.

The giant, rat-faced guy, whom Freya had assumed was Te Wiata's right-hand-asshole, walks to the head of the line. The spotty puppet walks up to him with a grin, looking like he's prepared something toady to say, but that just gets him shoved away.

"Who is that guy?" Freya whispers to Red.

"That's Doss. Every bit the thug Te Wiata is," Red whispers back, "but with none of the neurons."

The pale colossus stands, legs apart and arms crossed, in a heroic posture, facing the occupants of the accelerator pad. "You know what to do," he says in a bass register. "You ask where Prasad is. If they say they don't know or say they won't tell you, you shoot them dead. Right there. Don't even think twice. Then move on." This gets a giggle from some of the Allfours, which Doss ignores. "Got it?" he yells, taking Freya off guard.

The Allfours dare no hesitation. "Got it."

With this, Doss steps onto the pad.

FIFTY

There's distant gunfire echoing in the woods. Max, Joad, and security personnel march ahead of Dart and Kaira as they ascend the forest path towards the west campus. There are no TMA out there, so the Allfours must be shooting at nothing, or at each other. Or maybe the west campus is already under attack. Dart considers just how different these security guards are from him. His had been a life of science, at least up to his phase of folly. This had been his lens, his strength, his limitation. But these guys must inhabit a different world. He can tell they're trained in situational awareness. Something about the way they're scanning their environment. It's somehow not the way he'd do it. While he's just looking for any son-of-a-bitch Allfour with a gun, these guys are creating mental models of their surroundings, each sign of movement or sound in the woods a data point that instantly cues reallocation, widening or narrowing their attention based on some kind of spatial reasoning. And he guesses that they had coordinated their roles even before setting out. They must know what they're doing, and so his strategy is to fire or run in the same direction they do.

The gunfire is getting closer, but it sounds like random bursts rather than a concerted attack. He checks behind him and Kaira's face is stony. Behind her are two more security. Out of nowhere the guard following Kaira falls to the ground. In the blur of the instant, the thing that had hit him looked like a revolving stick.

"Down," shouts the rear guard and the squad drops to the ground. The fallen guard is staring up at the sky, wide-eyed, with an axe embedded in his neck. The rear guard takes off into the trees and Joad runs back, kneeling by the victim, and begins applying pressure on either side of the blade's line of entry. The blood spurts in pulses, too heavy to staunch. Then they hear a single shot, and they wait.

"A loner. Looked like one of the archaics who'd lost his way," the returning guard says.

Max places a hand on Joad's back. "You can't help him." The fallen guard's eyes are open but lifeless, and a stream of dark blood is running down the slope. "We keep moving."

Dart takes a deep, trembling breath to steady himself. He'd seen death by blade many times before. It had a special brutality to it—a reminder that people, in the end, are meat. He pulls the axe from the victim's neck and throws it to the ground.

"Let's go," Kaira says, bringing Dart back into the moment.

They crawl on their elbows to the crest of the slope. It's now clear that the intermittent bursts of gunfire are coming from the far side of it. They look over the top and down at the open field that descends to the west campus.

"Fuck almighty," Max says. The slope is covered by Te Wiata's ragbag army. Maybe half of them are Allfours and the rest are a cross-temporal mélange of what Dart assumes are mercenaries. They're not in ranks or anything else that hints at organization, but are standing in groups, talking, laughing, yelling. As far as Dart can make out, the mercenaries are archaics, although he couldn't begin to place them all. Most are Viking-esque for sure, but a few look like they've been plucked from other places and eras. It's clear that Te Wiata avoided arming his mercenaries with modern weapons. That at least seems like a quark of reason next to a planet of insanity.

Joad shakes his head. "He's completely out of his mind."

"Maybe," Max says. "I think he's going for chaos. Every bullet a mercenary takes is one less in an Allfour. And when you've got that many of them, they can do their own damage, even with blades."

Dart scrutinizes Max. She's talking about the man she loves ... isn't she? How can that not be a problem at some point? But there's nothing to reveal that in her eyes, her voice. "At least they're not assaulting the campus," he says. "Not yet."

Joad nods. "How many security do we have down there?"

"A dozen, maybe," Max replies.

Dart sees no sign of guards behind the fence.

"Shit. How long could they hold out?" Joad asks.

"It's not what I'd call a typical assault scenario, Joad. Depends on their strategy, if they have one. If it's a pitched battle and these assholes are committed, then maybe thirty minutes, tops. Too many bodies and armed Allfours to defend the perimeter any longer."

"And to get to Prasad?" Joad asks.

Max shrugs. "That depends on how cooperative our staff decide to be. When you have a sword to your groin, you might have less of a commitment to keeping secrets."

"Something's jamming us," one of the guards says. "I can't contact them down there."

"Ideas?" Joad asks.

"No way we're getting through them to the fence line," Max says. "They'd cut us down in seconds. Probably kill more of each other than us, but we wouldn't be around to scoff at that."

"Sooner or later they're going to get the order to attack," Joad says.

"And we're just going to watch the show from up here?" Kaira asks. "If they get to my grandfather then everything changes. Everything."

Max spits out some dirt. "We fucking know that, Princess."

FIFTY-ONE

Dense forest surrounds Freya and the air is floral and damp.

"With me," Doss barks at Sarah, who shoves Freya ahead of her. Uninvited, Red keeps pace. Doss pushes aside the disoriented Allfours who had arrived along with them. Eventually, the chatter of Allfours seems distant, and dappled light begins to break through the thinning trees. An Allfour Freya doesn't recognize appears out of the woods.

"Mr. Doss," he calls out. Behind him are a man and a woman in T-shirts and jeans. They are disheveled and covered in twigs, needles, and leaves. Another Allfour follows them, rifle in hand. "Found these two in the act."

Doss doesn't look at the captives but instead glares at the Allfour who had spoken to him. The man seems to transition rapidly from expecting a congratulatory pat to wondering how he'll be injured.

Freya can't help but smile. How bad can someone's timing be? The moment you pick for a little daytime delight is right when a shit-ton of Allfours pop out of nowhere.

"Did you ask them?" Doss whispers dangerously. The two Allfours stare back at him stupidly, and then at each other. The female Allfour's eyes reveal the moment of comprehension.

"Do you know where Prasad is?" she asks the male captive.

"Prasad?" He seems confused, as if he had been asked the whereabouts of Abraham Lincoln. The Allfour looks at Doss who says nothing. She shoots the man in a burst of fire and he's thrown against his partner, both of them toppling to the ground. The woman screams.

Freya gasps. "They're not going to just tell everyone about Prasad, even if he really is here."

Sarah slaps Freya across the face with a force that causes her to stagger backwards. "Enough from you, Momma's girl." Doss's attention had not been diverted from the Allfours.

"How about you?" the Allfour says promptly to the woman lying under her partner, his blood soaking her T-shirt. "Do *you* know where Prasad is?" The woman is too catatonic to speak, which earns her a round in the head.

"Was that so difficult?" Doss asks with the air of a schoolteacher. "To follow simple instructions?"

Sarah drags Freya forward. They leave the two Allfours standing over their victims, stepping back to avoid the rivulets of blood. Freya doesn't know what she's feeling. It should be horror and revulsion, but that's not it. It's alarm that she's not feeling those things. It's fright at the thought that she's becoming acclimatized to these obscene acts—to violent death. It's dismay that, at some level, Te Wiata's foul theory of every human's net moral neutrality has become an algorithm running in the background of her consciousness.

It takes Freya by surprise when the buildings come into view. There, on a lake shore beyond the edge of the wooded area, is a collection of structures—some of gleaming glass and steel reflecting sunlight into her eyes, and some of windowless concrete.

What the hell is this place?

It's a gleaming mini-city on the shore of a scenic lake,

whose inhabitants take sex excursions into the woods. Wherever this is, it can't be hell. At least not before these assholes arrived.

"Listen to me," Doss says into Freya's face. This would have been the time for a smart-ass, dismissive response for anyone else—even for Te Wiata—but not for this violent bastard, especially with Sarah behind her. "That glass building is where we know the Prasad girl was acceled to. We're going in there and we're going to find her. When we do, we're going to ask her where Prasad is. You're going to tell her to answer us. Because if she doesn't, or if she says she doesn't know, then you die on the spot. One bullet. Simple enough for you?"

"Why do you think she's going to give up her grandfather just because I ask?"

"Because," Sarah interjects, "she knows we'll find him anyway, and maybe she'll want to save her dyke girlfriend's life. And if she doesn't, that's fine too."

Doss turns away. "Copy that," he says into his headset. "Be on standby." He turns back to Freya and adds, "Seems some of the TMA vermin have scurried into a bunker. But we'll find her."

There are maybe a hundred Allfour troops ahead of them, and the same number behind. And unless Freya's losing her mind, there seems to be a smattering of archaic types among them, although they must be Allfours who are just too rakish to give up their fancy dress. Red gives Freya an unconvincing *it'll all be okay* nod.

Sarah shoves Freya forward as the Allfours ahead split into two columns. Some seem to be heading for one of the large concrete structures, and Freya is pushed to follow the others toward the glass building.

Is that a tomato? Freya shakes her head. Wouldn't it be hilarious if this were all an epic dream and she woke up at her desk in her university office looking at the back of

Damian's stupid head? Yes, it's a tomato. The dream scenario is the only thing that would make sense at this point.

Time travel? What bullshit.

Someone opens fire and several large panes of glass in the building ahead shatter. Doss yells something and there's deadly silence. Some excitable Allfour is in deep shit.

Crouched troops approach the main entrance to the glass building, and emboldened by the lack of any defensive action, the vanguard begins to stream in. Minutes pass and there's intermittent gunfire from inside. Through the glass walls she sees the Allfours navigating their way around, ascending staircases, kicking in doors. One walks up to a window, smiling brazenly and waving down to his friends on the ground.

"Simpletons, every one of them," Red says. Even Sarah stays quiet on that. Freya hears Doss muttering something behind her. She guesses this isn't his proudest moment. Then he stands up straight, looking down on his crouched army, and points at one of the two large concrete structures.

"Redirect," he shouts, and his troops slowly rise to follow him.

"Not you," Sarah hisses at Freya and pulls her back with a sharp tug.

"What the fuck is it with you?" Freya shakes off Sarah's hand, which earns her the look of someone considering whether now is the time for the violence they've always had in mind.

"She didn't tell you?" Red asks.

"Tell me what?"

Red smirks. "You didn't tell her?"

Sarah's eyes are wide with loathing.

"I guess you didn't. I suppose I didn't tell you either, Freya. That fact is, Sarah here and I were once engaged to be married."

Freya takes a moment to absorb this. "When?"

"Before you showed up. There were slim pickings in

Risley, and a secret office romance is always easier than bar-crawling or paying for it." Freya locks eyes with him. "Not you and me, Freya."

Sarah takes out a pistol and points it at Red.

He puts his hands up. "Really? You're going to shoot me? That'd be a low even for *our* relationship."

"Such an arrogant little shit. You think you've got anything to do with anything?" Sarah hisses. "This bitch is a TMA spy and you—"

"A lesbian spy, don't forget," Freya says. Sarah swings her gun from Red to Freya.

"Don't hate her," Red says. "If it makes you feel any better, I was already revolted by you before Freya ever showed up. I was thinking you'd be a good recruit for the Movement. But once I realized you really had a third-rate mind and were as funny as a tumor, well, not so much." Freya looks back and forth between them. "And the sex didn't help." It seems to her like a coupling made in heaven. "Besides, you know you're not going to harm Freya. I think Barry might react poorly to that."

All three of them jump as the shock wave passes through. There's smoke rising from the front of the concrete structure, and then the gunfire begins.

"If Kaira's in there they're going to kill her," Freya says.

"Doss won't let that happen," Red replies. "No one's going to risk having their bowels acceled out of them." Freya looks at Sarah, whose attention is on the pitched battle inside the bunker. They could easily take her right now. They could turn that gun on her while all these imbeciles are mesmerized by what's happening over there. No one is looking at them.

Without turning, Sarah raises the barrel of her handgun to Freya's head.

FIFTY-TWO

"If we could get our hands on some of those chic Allfours fatigues we could get down there unnoticed," Dart says.

"Maybe," Joad replies. "How do we do that?"

A shadow moves rapidly over the milling horde and Dart looks up. "Shit. Have you seen one fly that low before?"

"No."

"All of these goings-on must have made it curious," Max says. The giant bird then disappears over the trees behind them.

"Or," Joad says, "maybe they never saw anything worth coming down for before. This might look like a smorgasbord to them."

When the shouting and pointing begins, it's obvious that the bird hasn't gone unnoticed. Then the creature reappears from behind the trees. It's flying even lower now, maybe a hundred feet above them, and Dart can get his first detailed view. It's jet black but for a pink, unfeathered head, with a wingspan of maybe thirty feet. As it glides down the slope, its interest looks like more than idle curiosity. It emits a low-pitched scream from its long, sharp beak and dives at its first victim. The archaic is plucked from the ground by the massive talons and he flails in an almost vertical ascent.

Shouting has turned to shrieking as the Allfours and their mercenaries run chaotically in every direction, colliding, pushing, and falling over each other. There's gunfire, although no shots are landing on the bird, which flies away effortlessly with its struggling prey. Then a second bird appears and glides over the slope while, high in the sky, a flock congregates. It seems word has gotten out. In ones, twos, and threes, they descend like missiles as the flock grows. Within seconds, what had been a bright, cloudless sky is darkened, and the field of panicked raiders falls into shadow. If there's any gunfire, it's drowned out by the piercing shrieks of these flying monsters plucking men and women from the ground like treats. Some struggle enough to get free and plummet back down, only to be grabbed again and lifted into the darkened sky.

Max shouts to be heard above the din, but Dart can't make out what she's saying. She's pumping her thumb over her shoulder, and then begins to run back into the woods. The others follow and they all dive to the ground under the safety of tree cover.

It takes only minutes for the birds to clean their plate and for the cacophony to subside, diminishing to the intermittent and distant squawk of the receding raptors. The TMAers crawl back up to the ridge and look down towards the campus. The slope has been picked clean of humans. There are a few carcasses of downed birds, one of them fluttering its huge wings in its death throes. Then its wings collapse and there's only silence. The sun is visible again and the ocean behind the campus sparkles like a picture postcard, innocent of the horror that had occurred.

"Did that just happen?" Kaira asks. The birds vanished as quickly as they had appeared.

"Who the living fuck thought of putting Tomatotown here?" Dart asks as he stares into the sky.

"It's not perfect," Joad answers with the hint of a smile.

Max stands and takes a few strides down the slope. "Seems we can get down there now," she says.

"Really?" Dart replies. "You feel confident they're not in the mood for dessert?"

"Not seeing anything."

"They showed up pretty damn fast, Max." Dart looks down at the west campus structures behind the fence.

"It's only a matter of time before the next batch of Te Wiata's bird feed shows up," Joad says, "and they may not be dumb enough to just mill around before going in for the attack. We need to get down there while we can."

"Agreed," Max says. "Okay, we descend in lateral formation, twenty-foot spacing between us. It looked to me like it was the clustering that whet Big Bird's appetite."

"You're an ornithologist now?" Kaira says.

Max opens her mouth to respond, and from her expression, Dart senses it'll be something massively disproportionate.

"Keep looking up," he says before Max can continue. "My gut tells me that'll be a wise precaution."

They set off, eyes scanning the skies. A distant squawk gets everyone's attention, but there's nothing up there to be seen. Dart had experienced many flavors of dread across the ages, but this is a new one—being fed to a nest of hungry hatchlings, squawking heads bobbing in competition for parts of him.

They're halfway down the slope when the shadow passes over them. They freeze and look up in time to see the tail of a solitary bird vanishing behind the trees at the top of the slope. "Pick up the pace," Max shouts. The fence line is about a hundred yards ahead, and Dart can see the CCTV camera. He jogs down with the rest, his attention split between the rocks and shrubs that could down him, and Kaira to his side.

Then a deep, resonant scream sends a high voltage jolt through his bones. He hears shouting and turns to see a bird descending, talons stretched wide, its razor beak and dead, black eyes lasered right on him. The squawk is punctuated by a loud hiss as the animal makes its final approach, talons opening even wider. He falls onto his rear as he's bringing up his weapon. The talons can't be more than ten feet away, and the bird seems to be decelerating in confident anticipation of the grab and ascent. Dart releases a burst of fire. There's a blast of cold air and then a blow to the head flattens him as the animal passes over before crashing to the ground. He looks back and sees the beast fluttering and rolling under the ebbing strength of its giant wings.

It takes a moment to register what he's seeing beyond the dying raptor. Max is airborne and flailing, clasped in talons. He aims. Without conscious thought, he transitions to optimization. Sure, he could miss and kill her, but if he doesn't fire, then she's hatchling food, and if he fires too late, the fall will be fatal. He aims at the bird's head where he could afford a near miss. The animal's head explodes and it falls, talons frozen around its prey.

The flock is already reforming. Joad and one of the security are firing at a bird that's on the ascent, trying to take a guard with it. She's struggling in its claws and her weapon falls to the ground. The remaining two guards run down the slope with Kaira between them as two birds soar towards them, talons forward. Dart fires into them and they crash to the ground.

"She's gone," Joad shouts from behind him, and he turns to see his father and the guard running down the slope.

Max is back on her feet, firing into the descending flock. She's screaming something and Dart can faintly make out *big feathery fuckers*. He's in no mood to get on board with the obvious truth that they'll never get to the fence intact. He and Max are jogging backwards towards the fence, firing into the birds, some dropping to the ground and others ascending to take another run at their prey.

Then he notices something. Some of the birds are landing and ripping into their fallen kin, fighting each other over their meal. They've realized that this is a safer repast—

one that isn't spitting steel at them.

Dart and Max turn to make the final dash to the fence. The guards and Kaira are nowhere to be seen, which means they have either made it into the guardhouse or have been plucked from the ground. Max, Dart, Joad, and the remaining guard slam into the side of the guardhouse at the same instant and turn to fire into the oncoming squadron of raptors. Dart feels himself being grabbed from behind and he's the last to be dragged through the guardhouse door. Two guards then push their shoulders against the door, slamming it onto a set of talons that are opening and closing in a blind search for flesh. Max removes the handgun from her belt and shoots off the animal's foot as the guards finally force the door shut. The lock activates followed by the rapid, successive thuds of massive bodies slamming into the door. He looks up to see a flurry of feathers, claws, and heads banging into the reinforced glass as Kaira wraps her arms tightly around his neck.

FIFTY-THREE

Both ahead and behind, the column of Allfours extends as far as Freya can see, until it's obscured by the winding forest path. The screams echo inside her even now. It had started with rapid gunfire, and she'd imagined the occupants of the bunker trying to defend themselves against the torrent of Allfours through the smoking door. Then there had been silence followed by a single gunshot. She imagined the trapped TMAers being questioned, and as Doss had instructed, each wrong answer being rewarded with a bullet. The gunfire gradually accelerated and shouting had turned to screaming. It lasted for what seemed like an hour until a final volley of gunfire ended it. Without seeing a thing, Freya knew there had been a massacre, and the tears now streaming down her cheeks are ones of rage rather than sadness.

Freya's shivering, underdressed for the cold of falling darkness, and the handcuffs are cutting into her wrists. Sarah is behind her and hadn't spoken since they set out. Red is beside her, and each time she looks at him, he offers a smile intended to reassure, but no one could be less reassuring to her. At one point they step over a body that had had its throat opened, a battle-axe lying beside it. The victim is wearing the black uniform of TMA security. Red steps out of the column to pull the body from the path.

There's no conversation among the ranks other than the incomprehensible muttering of the ancients who, Freya had realized, are the real thing. Everyone knows what had just happened in that bunker, and while they may be impressionable idiots, they are human.

"So what happens if they find Prasad?" Freya asks Red. "Then what?"

He shakes his head. "I don't know. Te Wiata had us trying to kill his mother. I'm guessing he won't have a light touch."

"And what after that?"

"A bitch of a timeline shift, I suppose."

"But what does that even look like? Feel like?" If Sarah can hear this, she isn't acknowledging it. "What comes out the other side?"

She knows Red has no answers. She's pretty sure that no one does, even the madman who's about to make it happen. For him, the longshot of Te Wiata becoming the new Prasad is worth any risk.

There's someone standing to the side of the column, watching it pass. Freya notices the raspberry fingernails. Although she has a hundred quips competing to be said, she ignores the sitcom secretary. But the woman drags Freya to the side.

"What the hell?" Sarah says, but the secretary just keeps dragging until Freya finds herself in a grove of trees, a few yards from the column. Red is following at a distance.

The secretary's hard, blue eyes bore into Freya. "Why are you still alive?" the secretary asks.

Freya looks at Sarah, who's caught up with them, as if she were more equipped to answer the question. The secretary turns to Sarah. "You had orders." Sarah looks confused. "The TMA shitbags squealed. We know where Prasad is now so this one has no use. *That* order."

Sarah looks at Freya and then back at the secretary. "I never got that order."

"Well, you're getting it now."

"From you? When the fuck did you get to give me orders?"

The secretary raises her pistol to Freya's head, and her body suddenly feels like a block of ice, as if it had died in anticipation. Freya closes her eyes and holds her breath. A shot is fired and she winces. Her eyes open to see the secretary on the ground and Sarah checking to make sure the job had been done. Freya's brain takes a second to catch up with events and she begins to shake. Sarah is staring at her, expressionless, as if calculations are being executed. Then the Allfour slowly raises her pistol to Freya's head, and in a blur, something strikes Sarah's arm. She looks down at her severed limb, dangling from her by a thread of flesh. Red raises the axe for a second blow.

"No," Freya shouts. Sarah falls to her knees and looks up at Red in shock. He picks up the pistol.

"Do it," Sarah says. "Just do it." Red hesitates as if asking for Freya's permission.

"What's the code for the cuffs?" Freya asks. Sarah, who seems quite serene, recites four digits.

"Dying quick or dying slow are the only options for her," Red says as he removes the cuffs from Freya. She closes her eyes and nods, and even though it's expected, the shot makes her jump.

"She wasn't going to kill me, Red," Freya says.

"Did you want me to wait and be sure?"

They gather up the weapons and exit the grove of trees. It seems the passing column had taken the gunfire in its stride—just another Allfour shooting off a few rounds for no good reason. Freya rejoins the column and beckons Red to follow.

FALL OF TIME

This is the only way she'll find Kaira.

FIFTY-FOUR

Joad and Joon are leading the way. "How many security?" Joad asks the site director.

"With yours and Max, fifteen. How many of them are you guessing are out there?"

"You don't wanna know." They arrive back at the laboratory and look through the door window. The young Prasad and Te Wiata, as usual, are standing at a whiteboard and shaking their heads at each other. Kaira peers over Dart's shoulder.

"He looks like you expected?" Dart asks her. She studies her grandfather.

"I've seen enough images. But seeing him moving ... living ..." She smiles at Dart. "So I'm not allowed in there. Fucking TMA rules, right?"

Dart shrugs. He had accepted that everyone and everything is its own flavor of idiotic. He feels a hand on his shoulder that pulls him out of the way.

"Mind if I go in?" Max asks. Joon looks at Joad who nods. The young Te Wiata is deep in conversation and only notices Max when she throws her arms around him. There are two Maxs, Dart realizes: the one when she's with baby Te Wiata and the one when she isn't. And sometime soon, those Maxs will have to meet.

"Where can we protect him best?" Joad asks. Joon ponders it.

"We were never set up for this. This scenario was inconceivable." Dart knows when his father is irritated. It's in his smile. It seems the site director knows, too. "I'm sorry, Joad. There's nowhere safer than where he is right now. We could barricade this corridor. That'd hold them off for a while."

Holding them off for a while seems to be the best-case scenario. But what does that get them? It's not like the cavalry is on its way.

"Okay," Joad says. "Ten security on the site perimeter. Maybe if we put up a fight they'll get discouraged. But if the perimeter is breached, all security fall back to defend this space. Got it?" Joon nods.

"This is the only entry to the lab space, right? Get everyone in there."

"Everyone?"

"Can anyone use a gun?"

"A few, maybe."

"Then arm them and let them take direction from security. The rest, lock up in there."

Dart watches his father. Everything he'd learned about cynicism he'd learned from the best. Yet here the man is, full of ludicrous optimism and barking out orders. Fifteen security guards and a few poor bastards with guns thrust at them, including him, against the amassed army of a crazy Xerxes. Here, the boundary between optimism and delusion collapses.

With no chairs left to be had, Joad and Dart are sitting up against the wall in a corner of the lab. The scientists and engineers wait in silence at their benches. This is not what any of them had signed up for. Prasad and Te Wiata are among them. Neither man has been informed of their predicament, but they must know they're waiting for something. Something that's not good. It amuses Dart that even in these dire and terminal circumstances, TMA clings to its sacred fucking rules.

By now it must be dark outside, so Te Wiata's army is probably not even under the threat of the raptors. That's a shame. Those big hungry bastards would have made a good cavalry.

Dart could have been with Kaira in her hideout, but he wants to be by his father for a few more minutes. It's maybe his last chance.

"Are they here yet?" Dart asks.

"Oh yes. They're out there. Waiting."

"For what? How many?"

Joad shrugs. "Hard to know. Hundreds. If only a fraction of the arrivals are out there, that's plenty."

Dart knows his father could have tried to underplay their predicament, and he's pleased that Joad respects him enough not to do it. Dart looks across the room at Prasad, who's hunched over a bench, scribbling something. His brain never stops. Who can imagine what's being jotted on that pad? Maybe it's the first scribble of a whole new science.

"What does a timeline shift feel like?"

Joad flashes a smile at his son. "You ask me this now? You want *the birds and the bees* talk from your dad?" Dart grins. "But I guess now is a good time to ask." Joad takes a breath. "You know, theory has it that we go through shifts all the time and don't even notice—not even tuskers."

"I know. Timelines reconverging in the long run. But what if you're in the middle of one, before reconvergence? What's it like?"

"Nothing, Casy. Tuskers keep the memory of their timeline but find themselves in a new one. That's it."

Dart frowns. "But what about the memory of the new timeline? It comes with its own history, right? Where does that memory show up?"

Joad shrugs. "Truth is, Casy, we're clueless about most of the new physics. We're just infants trying to find our way." Joad nods towards Prasad. "Even him. Having the math down is not the same as understanding. It's a brave new world and we're all lost in it."

"And you've never been in the midst of a shift?" Dart glances up at Joad but it ends in a double-take. "What?"

Joad leans back against the wall. "I have been in the midst of one," he says.

Dart waits.

"Now's the time, I guess. Casy ... well ... I was married before I met your mom."

Dart blinks. "Say again?"

"It was in a different timeline, and then it shifted. You ask what it's like? It's like I'd been married for a decade but I actually hadn't. My memory didn't change—only the reality."

Dart stares at his father. "Who ... who was she?"

"It was not a good match. And a timeline shift is much less messy than a divorce." Dart doesn't smile. "No, It's not funny. And then after the shift, I met your mother. And that match was perfect."

A hundred questions course through Dart's mind, yet any one of them seems like a trivial place to start.

"You okay?" Joad whispers. Dart shrugs and his father pats his knee. "We may not have another chance, so there's one more thing."

"Holy shit, Joad. Something else? Really?" Dart holds his breath.

"Yeah. It's the tachyonic horizon mystery."

Dart exhales in relief. That's only science.

"That mystery is kind of close to my heart, Casy. It involves your mom."

"What? How?"

"Gallie was caught on the wrong side of it—on the other side of the horizon."

Dart feels a wave of nausea that starts deep in his

stomach and then rises through him. Joad continues, "She was sent forward just short of the horizon. And due to ... circumstances, she didn't get out in time. All it took was for the clock to just keep ticking forward at one second per second."

"Until she wound up on the wrong side of the horizon?"

Joad nods.

"How?"

"She was ... detained. A TMA team was on the trail of a tachyonic field anomaly, and it turns out an Allfours team was on the case too. Don't know details, but we're pretty sure they took away her ability to accel back, and the horizon just overtook her. Whoever put that shield up, they did it while she was there."

"Or she was killed."

"No. Putting TMA operatives on the far side of the horizon is an Allfours thing. It's another of Te Wiata's innovations. But we'll get her back," Joad says, squeezing Dart's knee.

"When we get out of this, you mean?"

Joad nods despite the irony. Dart takes a few deep breaths. He can feel his father looking at him but can't look back. "And if Te Wiata snuffs Prasad, how does it all shift?" he asks, although the question is more for himself than for Joad. "No TMA, no Joad meets Gallie, and so no me, I guess. Should be painless as far as I'm concerned, at least."

"A billion possible outcomes, Casy. You know that. And anyway, we're here to make sure that that question stays hypothetical."

Dart looks at the solitary guard standing by the lab entrance.

FIFTY-FIVE

The gibbous moon hangs low in the sky and is the only illumination. No lights are visible in the base, but Freya can make out a fence around its perimeter and a single structure within. The horde she's part of is milling around on the slope that descends to the base, and she can tell that some of the Allfours, equipped with headsets, are making plans.

She had been getting special attention from the ancients. It's unnerving to be weighed up by someone from an era of casual assault. There are several huge carcasses strewn about the slope that look like monstrous birds. One suddenly flutters a giant wing and the Allfours who had been inspecting it cry out.

Beyond the base, the moon is reflected in what looks like an ocean. It only just occurs to Freya to wonder where and when they are.

"What do you want to do?" Red asks.

"We need to get in there. It's where Kaira is."

"And Prasad."

"Of course." She looks at Red. It seems it's Team Freya/Red again. How did that happen? And how is he going to screw them both this time? What act of idiocy will seem to him like a good idea? And most painful of all, why, in this moment, doesn't she hate him?

Red looks back at her. He must think she's formulating a plan. He says, "We could—"

Her shoulders jump with the crack of the explosion. In the light of the ascending fireball, they see a small building on the perimeter of the base that has burst into flames.

She begins to run down the slope and Red follows, once he realizes she's no longer beside him. Then the gunfire starts and Freya throws herself to the ground. It lasts a matter of seconds before ebbing to random bursts that Freya now recognizes as Allfours exuberance. She looks back at Red, whose eyes are reflecting the inferno ahead. There are Allfours shouting at the approaching horde. They seem to be selecting who gets into the base. It makes sense. Someone with a mind to escape might find it easier amidst a mob. She runs forward and then feels a tight grip on her arm.

"Not you—" is what the Allfour gets out before the butt of Red's rifle knocks him sideways.

Once inside the perimeter, Freya and Red stop to take stock. Lit by the inferno that had been the guardhouse, they see Allfours clambering to get ahead of one another as they rush towards the single, central structure.

FIFTY-SIX

The walls shake with the explosion and Dart jumps to his feet. He looks at the guard, who nods. "That's our cue—let's join the team," Dart says to Kaira. "You avoid gramps, okay?"

"Would rather die than break a TMA rule," she replies. "And I think we're about to prove it." Dart grins, knowing they're thinking exactly the same thing.

It's just like the old days, and if they're both done for, then two Musketeers will burst into hell with a hail of bullets.

They assume a ready posture with their weapons, the guard kicks open the door, and they file out.

The gunfire is getting louder. There's no one out there for the Allfours to be shooting at, but it makes it easier to gauge their proximity. They dash down one corridor after another with the guard covering their rear. Dart stops at a corner and waves the others to line up flat against the wall. He shouts the watchword and receives acknowledgment. They turn the corner and up ahead are the armored partitions that are protecting the laboratory entrance. There are more partitions at the corners of the merging corridors, between them and the lab, and behind each are guards. One of them waves Dart forward.

He experiences a flash of optimism. Could these defenses work? At least no matter how many Allfours attack, they'll need to pass through this narrow channel, and maybe they'll be dumb enough to just keep on coming and let themselves get shot like tin ducks in a shooting gallery. The guard pushes open the lab door.

"I'm staying out here," Dart says.

"Me too," Kaira says.

"Hell no." She's not used to being told to keep out of the fray. She usually *is* the fray. "Please," he says. She hesitates and then kisses him before backing into the lab. He looks through the door window as Kaira turns and smiles at him. He thinks to smile back, but she's already gone. He motions some of the scientists inside to move out of the line of fire.

They wait. The gunfire is getting louder and there's a continuous crashing of glass.

What the hell can they be shooting at?

Then someone in fatigues appears from around the corner at the far end of the corridor. He looks stupidly at the partitions as if trying to figure out if they're friendly. A second Allfour dashes out and is raising her weapon when a burst of fire slams them both into the back wall. A silence follows except for hushed murmuring from around the corner. Dart looks along the sight of his rifle, his finger poised on the trigger. Sweat trickles into his eye and he wipes it away.

An arm swings around the corner, lobbing an object that rolls to a rest in front of one of the partitions. When it detonates, the partition and the guards behind it are launched in every direction, and then through the smoke, Dart sees the stampede of Allfours.

He opens fire along with all the TMA guards. The Allfours in the vanguard begin to fall, others tripping or jumping over them. Then dense red smoke begins to billow towards the lab. Dart fires into the smoke. The gunfire is now a continuous din without punctuation, and the guard beside Dart is thrown back against the lab door. The partition, not designed for this force of assault, is being driven back by the sheer pressure of the steel barrage. Feeling the draft of near misses on his cheeks, he drops to his knees as the guards flanking him fall. Then the door behind him opens and he rolls in.

Joad drags his son out of the line of fire as the wall opposite the entrance disintegrates into splinters, shards, and dust. The gun battle in the corridor continues for a few more seconds, although it may be only Allfours' fire, then abruptly stops. There's a brief silence, then banal yells of victory.

Dart scans the room. Some of the TMAers are huddled in the corners, with others crouched behind benches and equipment. A few of the scientists are holding weapons, terror in their eyes. Some are looking at him and Joad as if waiting for instructions. There's no sign of Prasad, young Te Wiata, or Kaira. But there's nowhere they could be hidden, and he imagines Max has them crouching behind something, a fresh clip in her rifle, ready to take a glorious last stand. That would be her style.

There's blood dripping from his hand, and he follows the stream back up to a gash on his forearm. He looks at the door to the lab, its glass blown out and clusters of bullet holes leaving more void than metal. He releases the box magazine from his rifle and replaces it. When they burst through that door, it's over. He knows that. He looks at his father and raises his eyebrows in resignation. Joad winks. He suddenly remembers that Joad used to wink at him. Not at anyone else, just at him. It was when they were sharing a secret. But what was going to happen next didn't seem like a secret.

Then they hear the voice. "Have we had enough of this?" Joad and Dart exchange a glance. "This is Barry and I'm calling time on this nonsense."

The TMAers have been corralled into a corner with a line of Allfours' rifles trained on them. There's no cowering, no simpering; the scientists just stare stoically at their captors. It's obvious that not just any TMAers had been picked to work here.

All eyes are on the remains of the door, waiting. Seconds pass.

Then Te Wiata enters. He sidesteps the pile of relinquished weapons and then, with ceremony, raises his head slowly towards his captives. He's more enormous than Dart remembers—the scale of a grizzly more than a man. Following him closely is the big ugly guy with livid skin, shaven head, and an expression of contempt that all of this took so much effort.

Te Wiata smiles. "And who's in charge of this crack unit?"

"I am," Dart hears Joad say from behind him. They clear an aisle and Joad comes forward. "I'm Joad Bevan."

Te Wiata's eyebrows arch. "*The* Joad Bevan," he says, looking at his angry lieutenant. "We're in the company of TMA royalty. This is the man who put paid to that miscreant Kasper Asmus." Te Wiata shakes his head. "Financial gain from time travel? Not acceptable. I wish I could have dealt with him myself, but Dr. Bevan here took care of it for us all."

Te Wiata continues to scan the TMA huddle. He stops at Dart. "I know you, don't I? Yes, I do. You're the skinny, young fellow who tried to mix it up in Glasgow." Again, he looks at his acned sidekick. "He may not look like much, but this chappy has some serious gonads on him." The lieutenant is unimpressed. "Well, what a gathering. What a gathering, indeed. Come, Joad Bevan. And you too, my Musketeer friend. Let's go and have a little chinwag."

FIFTY-SEVEN

The din of gunfire has been replaced by the inane yelling and laughter of Allfours as they wreck and loot the campus. In every office Freya and Red pass, there's equipment being smashed or carried off, some Allfours teaming up to hoist their more unwieldy finds.

Freya and Red turn onto one corridor after another to see the same thing, and the acrid, sweet smell of ammunition propellant is getting stronger. Then, through wisps of red smoke, Freya sees it. It takes a moment to register that what she's seeing is a pile of bodies at the far corner of the corridor. She's frozen by the sight. Red walks ahead until he reaches the corner, his back to the wall, and peeks around it. Then he shakes his head, signaling for her to stay back. *You don't want to see this.* Ignoring Red had become her primary form of interaction, so she strides past him.

It's carnage. Bodies layered deep, open-eyed, blown apart, some still bleeding out. They're mostly Allfours, but there are TMA security among them. The scene is haloed by tendrils of red smoke and the air is dense with the sickly stench of propellant. There's a solitary Allfour leaning against the wall. He seems bemused, disconnected.

"What happened here?" Freya asks. The Allfour just stares, dead-eyed. At the end of the corridor, beyond the carnage, there's a room in which she sees motion.

"You don't want to go in there," the Allfour says. "Things are going to happen in there." He spits into a pool of blood and drags his sleeve across his mouth. "You don't want to go in there." Freya waits for the explanation, and realizing it's not coming, wades forward. "You want to know what happened here?" the Allfour calls after her. "Madness. That's what."

Freya and Red approach what's left of the door, which is ragged with gunshot. They stand on either side of the opening, weapons poised. The voice is Te Wiata's—unmistakably. But there's no one in view, just the voice.

"Drop those," they hear from behind. The Allfour seems to have snapped out of his melancholy. She looks at Red and shakes her head. He's just dumb enough to go for it. Their rifles clatter to the ground, and then their pistols. "Go on. You don't want to take my advice. If you're so curious, step inside. See what happens."

Freya and Red exchange a glance like tragic lovers on a cliff edge. They raise their hands and step inside.

Doss and his Allfours are surrounding a clutch of people squashed into a corner. Some of their weapons are redirected at Freya and Red as they enter the lab.

"This is a surprise," Freya hears, and she turns to see Te Wiata. With him are the skinny Musketeer along with another man she thinks she recognizes from somewhere.

"This is quite the Musketeers reunion," Te Wiata says. "Come." Freya navigates the haphazard arrangement of lab benches and computer terminals. There's no sign of Kaira.

She notices that Dart is bleeding, a trail of blood spotting the path he must have taken. "But there seems to be a Musketeer missing." Te Wiata feigns concern. "Where is my beautiful Kaira? And my good friend, her grandfather?"

Silence.

Te Wiata removes the pistol from his belt, cocks it, and shoots Red. Despite herself, Freya cries out and falls to her knees beside him. Te Wiata looks at the familiar TMAer and says, "I just needed to do that before I forget."

"Enough, Te Wiata," the TMAer says. "Enough."

Doss has now joined them, knowing where the action lies.

"Look," Te Wiata says, "we can drag this out if you like, but I know he's here, and you know I'll find him. The only real question is how many of you do you want me to kill in the meanwhile?"

The TMAer and Dart shoot a look at each other.

"Okay, Max," the TMAer says in little more than a whisper. A wall panel pivots softly to the floor. Standing behind it is Kaira along with two others. She looks unharmed. She glances at Freya without acknowledging her. One of the others is a woman who's as tall as Freya, with blond hair and creepily pale eyes. The third one is a tall, slender guy who …

It's Te Wiata. No question. Younger, trimmer, thick black hair and looking completely bewildered, but no question—those are the features buried deep in the old Te Wiata. She's seeing the same man twice … next to himself.

It floods Freya afresh with the insanity of it all.

The three of them step forward. Te Wiata seems at a loss for words. That's a first—not in complete control. To see a younger self must do that to a person, but then Freya notices that it's not the young Te Wiata who's having this effect on him.

"Maxine," Te Wiata whispers. The blond woman stares at him. The silence is long enough for Doss to look at his boss with concern. "A surprise." He looks at her for a moment longer, then gathers himself before turning to his young self. "Well, I now see my fondness for the finer things has had an effect." The young version just stares, open-mouthed. "And my beautiful Kaira. As radiant as ever."

Kaira ignores this and steps forward to be beside Dart.

"But someone's missing. Kaira, where's my friend, Ram?"

The question is stupidly casual, as if it might trick Kaira into answering.

"What do you think you're going to do?" the familiar TMAer says. "You're Barry Te Wiata. No one understands better than you that, whatever you have in mind, the consequences are unknowable." A faint smile appears on Te Wiata's lips. "For fuck's sake, Te Wiata. Get sane."

"Where is he?" Te Wiata waits. "If you don't produce him, the consequences of *that* are knowable."

The TMAer looks at something beyond Te Wiata, and Freya turns. A diminutive Indian man walks slowly towards them. From a thousand images, Freya knows she's seeing Ramesh Prasad.

"Are you looking for me?" His voice is soft and high-pitched.

Kneeling over Red, Freya positions her hand above the wound in his stomach, not daring to touch it. Red winces and pulls up his blood-soaked shirt. At first, it seems he's trying to expose the wound, but then she sees it. It's an axe head sticking out from the side of his waistband. Their eyes lock and he nods weakly.

"Ram," Te Wiata murmurs. Freya senses that Te Wiata had not correctly predicted his own reaction, and his attempt to smile fails in an ugly grimace.

But Te Wiata doesn't have Prasad's attention. Instead, the small man is looking at Kaira. The smile on Prasad's face grows as he approaches her.

"My god," Prasad whispers, and then sweeps Kaira up into his arms. They're about the same height, and in a tight embrace, each rests their head on the other's shoulder. Prasad's eyes are shut tight and there are tears rolling down his cheeks.

And there's something ... Freya isn't sure ... something ... Prasad is not letting go of his granddaughter and his shoulders begin to shake. What that *something* is occurs to Freya. How did Prasad recognize his granddaughter? He can't have met her before—not his future grandchild. She knows that Kaira had never met *him*. A family resemblance, maybe? No, the moment of recognition had overwhelmed him. If he had ...

Freya stops breathing.

That's not who she is. No logic could have pointed her to it, yet she knows it. In Prasad's face is something she understands. In that moment, Freya knows that she had once saved Kaira's life—in that Vancouver tenement.

Kaira isn't Prasad's granddaughter.

FIFTY-EIGHT

Maa is the word Prasad had used. He had whispered it, but Dart is sure of what he'd heard.

He can see Kaira's face over Prasad's shoulder. She's disoriented. Her arms have dropped to her sides, but Prasad still has a tight hold on her. Dart looks to see if anyone understands what's happening. Joad appears lost in thought—the look he has when he's considering his options. Freya looks unnerved, staring at Kaira and Prasad. Athos is busy nursing the hole in him. And Te Wiata is wide-eyed.

It hits like a hammer blow. Dart needs to reframe everything he knows, and he needs to do it quickly.

Is this what a timeline shift feels like? But no, this is no reality shift; it's a shift in his comprehension. Retrieving Kaira had been so critically important to Joad. And what naivety to think it had all been about the sentimental mission of rescuing Prasad's granddaughter.

That wasn't it. It had all been about protecting the timeline. Kaira was every bit as important as Prasad himself. If she were eliminated ...

Kaira backs away from Prasad, and Max takes a step forward, putting herself between Kaira and Te Wiata.

Te Wiata grins. "I'm not often surprised," he whispers. "All I can say is *well done*, Dr. Joad Bevan, well done, TMA. Well done, indeed." He turns to Prasad. "You fooled me all along. Who you become fooled me, that is. You put little Kaira on my lap and introduced me to your granddaughter. But it was all about you. All about protecting you—protecting the sacred timeline. I was never in the loop, was I? Never trusted."

Te Wiata looks at Joad. "Then what a terrible shock it must have been when the beautiful Kaira runs off with the rebels. But I should call her Noor Agarwal now, shouldn't I?" Te Wiata chuckles and shakes his head. "TMA had lost the great Prasad's mother. Let her slip through its fingers." He guffaws loudly and then looks down at Red. "I'm guessing our TMA friends plucked baby Agarwal right after your incompetent attempt to deal with her." He turns to Freya. "With a little help from the spy?"

Dart takes a step towards Kaira, but Te Wiata's thug places a hand on his chest and shoves him hard. The young Te Wiata looks like he's about to come to Dart's defense but Max grabs his arm.

Kaira had been silent. She begins to shake her head. "No." She looks at Prasad. "No, that's—"

"But yes," Te Wiata says. "Your own son didn't trust you. Hurts, doesn't it?" Te Wiata puts an arm around Prasad's shoulder and beckons Kaira towards him. "I think it's time for a few words in private."

Kaira glances at Dart and then steps forward. With a meaty arm around each of them, Te Wiata leads Prasad and Kaira away in a ludicrous juxtaposition of human scale: a giant between two Lilliputians. Adrenaline courses through Dart. *It's over if Te Wiata takes them away. But it's over anyway, isn't it? The shift is inevitable. A shift to god knows what.*

Te Wiata stops and pulls the two slight figures around to face him. They begin to exchange words that Dart can't hear.

Red groans and Dart looks down. Freya is staring up at

him, her eyes motioning toward something. There's an axe tucked down the side of Red's pants.

They've stopped talking. Kaira's lips hint at a smile for Dart as Te Wiata removes the pistol from his holster and takes a step back. He points the gun at Prasad.

Freya's scream is unintelligible as she rips the axe from Red's waist and tosses it to Dart, head-first.

Te Wiata turns. He roars "No," turning the pistol on Dart.

The pale thug is raising his rifle when Max throws herself into him, causing him to lurch sideways and take Te Wiata's bullet in the face. Dart releases a guttural scream, and with all the strength in him, he swings the axe blade into the young Te Wiata's throat. Someone cries out but Dart doesn't know who.

FIFTY-NINE

The sunlight is blinding. Dart shuts his eyes and his inner eyelids are electric blue. It takes a moment to feel the hand on his shoulder. He shields his eyes as he slowly opens them. This is the bench overlooking the lake in front of the main Tomato building. The lake's surface is still and glittering.

"You okay?" It's Joad voice. Dart nods without turning.

A shadow passes over them and Dart looks up to see a solitary high flyer. "You'd asked me what a timeline shift feels like, Casy. Feels like nothing." Dart nods again. He looks over his shoulder. The tomato is still there. "You took a risk," Joad says. "Hell of a risk on how much Te Wiata mattered."

"A risk? You think it was that well-calculated?"

Joad smiles. "Yes, I do."

Dart stands and draws a deep breath. The air is light and fragrant. He looks at his arm and there's no wound. His legs tremble and he sits back down. "Now what?"

"Now, I find out what's what. What's the same. What's not. It's the burden of a tusker." Joad looks at his son. "And you. Time for you to figure a few things out, I think. Decide what's next for Casy Bevan."

Dart shrugs. "What do *you* think should be next for Casy

Bevan?"

"I like this timeline already. One in which you care what I think."

Dart looks into the distance. "I think I want to stay."

"And Kaira—"

"I know. You don't have to tell me about Kaira." He looks at his father and a smile flickers across his face. "There's a plan bigger than me. Bigger than me and Kaira. Or are you going to tell me I'm Prasad's father?"

Joad shakes his head and smiles. "No."

"No," Dart echoes.

"I want you working with me," Joad says in a whisper. "I can't tell you that TMA has it all figured out. Maybe the 4th Movement has something right. They're undisciplined and incompetent, and we're reactionary and inflexible. I don't know where truth lies, where right lies. Maybe the universe is telling us what reality is, but TMA is trying to stick to rules that only made sense in the old world. Maybe we're treating *One Second per Second* as a law handed down by the Almighty and not just an artifact of outdated science. It's too big to wrap a mind around yet. But something I do know is that TMA is just trying to do the right thing. That's what I can hold on to for now. And I'd like you with me."

There's the hum of a motor and Dart turns to see a small boat approaching the pier. "You think that's Max?"

Joad nods. "Shall I come with you?"

Dart shakes his head. This has to be his conversation. He stands and sets off down the pier.

Max's expression is blank as she pulls the boat parallel to the jetty and lassos a docking post. He steadies the boat and Max steps onto the pier. They look at each other and there are no words. He places a hand on her arm. Her nod is almost imperceptible, but it washes over Dart. Max's attention shifts and Dart looks over his shoulder. Joad is still at the top of the pier, but he isn't facing them. He's looking at someone standing beyond him.

Dart shivers. He feels Max's hand on his shoulder as he

watches his parents approach one another.

SIXTY

Freya enters the barn to see Red patting Penelope. The ruddy hue she remembered has returned to his cheeks.

"Dart loved this old thing," he says. "He loved this whole place."

"What about you, Red?" Freya asks. "Do you love it? Enough to stay?"

Red ponders it. "Maybe. Some great memories here. I suppose I have some decisions ahead."

Freya nods. There's no doubt that there had been a timeline shift—that she'd been at its epicenter. A few tackynet communications revealed that TMA is strong and thriving, as are the Allfours in their chaotic, anarchic kind of way. Of course, finding herself in 1960s northern England had been her first clue. "You have options, Red. You can stick with the Allfours—maybe it's too late for the Musketeers but you could form a tribute band." Red chuckles. "Or you could go back to TMA. I think they'd take you. Or—"

"Or?"

"Or you could get a real fucking job."

Red laughs. "And what about Freya the Dragon Slayer? Where does she go from here?"

Freya pats Penelope's soft hide. "Going to spend some time with the family, but after that, I'm not sure. There's something in me that wants to return to the quiet life of academia. Stop the tachyon surfing; trying to control the uncontrollable, comprehend the incomprehensible."

"So, just churning out middling students and papers no one reads?"

"Ha. I know. Who am I kidding?" Penelope's big brown eyes turn on Freya as if in agreement. "Jenn wants me back in Risley. Joad offered me a job in Tomatotown. I have options, I guess."

Freya knocks on the bedroom door and enters. There are still the faint stains of Porthos's blood on the floorboards, but Kaira had insisted on sleeping in the room that had been hers and Dart's. Kaira looks lost in an oversized woolen sweater and her hands are tucked deep into her jeans. If it were a degree colder, their breath would be visible, but no one has been in the mood to build a fire.

"What's the word?" Freya asks.

Kaira takes her hand. The emotions that that would once have inflamed are now gone. Events are bigger than her. Bigger than Kaira. There had been a play in which Freya had been lucky enough to land a small part. But now Kaira is moving on to a new production that has no role for Freya.

She pulls Kaira towards her, hugs her for a moment, then lets go.

"Vancouver, 1941," Kaira whispers. "Seems there's a man I'm destined to meet."

Freya smiles. "When?"

"Today." Kaira runs a thumb over Freya's cheek. Perhaps she'd seen a tear, but Freya hadn't felt it.

Then Red enters the bedroom and whispers transition to banter.

"So, Athos. Decided yet?" Kaira asks.

"Okay, party trick. Give me a year," he says to his fellow

Musketeers. "And it can be 1964."

Kaira grins. "1964."

"Oh, that's the year Red Bakker gets back into the family business—Penelope and I have big plans. We're going to invent sustainable agriculture, and way ahead of the curve. We're turning this place into a going concern."

ACKNOWLEDGEMENTS

For me, writing is a family business. I thank my wife, Heather, who is always my first reader, and spot-on with her suggestions. My son, Stephen, created the book cover, and my son, Gareth, was in my head as I wrote one of the characters. Although not related to me, Erika Steeves was my copyeditor and did a first-rate job.

ABOUT THE AUTHOR

S. D. Unwin started out as a theoretical physicist searching for the Holy Grail of a quantum theory of gravity. He later turned his mathematical skills to analyzing and communicating catastrophic risk, from nuclear mishaps to major earthquakes. He has now settled happily on writing science fiction. Hailing originally from Manchester in the United Kingdom, Bainbridge Island in Puget Sound is where he calls home.

SDUnwin.com

Follow on Facebook:
facebook.com/unwinbooks

Also by S. D. Unwin

The Magni

The One Second Per Second Time Travel Trilogy:

One Second Per Second
Fall Of Time
Time Wall

Printed in Dunstable, United Kingdom